KEEPING HER SAFE

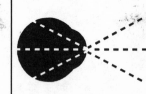

This Large Print Book carries the
Seal of Approval of N.A.V.H.

KEEPING HER SAFE

BARBARA PHINNEY

THORNDIKE PRESS

A part of Gale, Cengage Learning

GALE
CENGAGE Learning™

Detroit • New York • San Francisco • New Haven, Conn • Waterville, Maine • London

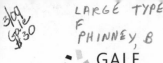

3 1257 01809 2352

Copyright © 2008 by Barbara Phinney.
Thorndike Press, a part of Gale, Cengage Learning.

Thorndike Press® Large Print Christian Mystery.
The text of this Large Print edition is unabridged.
Other aspects of the book may vary from the original edition.
Set in 16 pt. Plantin.
Printed on permanent paper.

LIBRARY OF CONGRESS CATALOGING-IN-PUBLICATION DATA

Phinney, Barbara.
    Keeping her safe / by Barbara Phinney.
        p. cm. — (Thorndike Press large print Christian mystery)
    ISBN-13: 978-1-4104-1327-7 (alk. paper)
    ISBN-10: 1-4104-1327-6 (alk. paper)
    1. Ex-convicts—Fiction. 2. Secrecy—Fiction. 3. Large type books. I. Title.
PS3616.H48K44 2009
813'.6—dc22   2008045454

Published in 2009 by arrangement with Harlequin Books S.A.

Printed in the United States of America
1 2 3 4 5 6 7 13 12 11 10 09

Therefore, there is now no condemnation for those who are in Christ Jesus.

— *Romans* 8:1

To my family and friends and church, who put up with my weird writing moments and risk getting put into a book. All of you are the greatest!

ONE

Rae Benton could not believe who had just walked into the mortuary chapel. The man who'd killed her father had the gall to attend his victim's funeral.

With hands clenched as tightly as her jaw, she lifted her gaze from the inexpensive casket, up Hunter Gordon's lean frame to meet his eyes. In the muted light, she couldn't see the vivid blue, just the intensity that carried both empathy and wariness. She could buy the wariness; after all, he couldn't expect to be welcomed here. But empathy? Hunter might not have pulled a trigger, but he *was* responsible for her father's untimely death. He had no right to show any compassion.

He came to stand near her. "I'm sorry, Rae." His voice had deepened during his years in prison, yet she could barely hear it in the quiet chapel. His words were obviously meant for her alone. "I wish I could have been here sooner."

"Because you've just been released?" she muttered. "How did you get here so fast? Dorchester Penitentiary is a two-hour drive from here. They don't release inmates at dawn."

"I hitched a ride with a guard coming off duty."

"Who told you Dad had died?"

His compassionate expression faltered slightly, but his voice stayed calm. "We stopped for gas up the road. The clerk told me. I came straight here."

Edith Waterbrook owned the only gas station in the small New Brunswick village of Green Valley. Which meant if she'd recognized Hunter after ten years, everyone would soon know he'd been released. And had headed straight to the funeral.

Rae found herself fighting back the conflicting urges to smack him, and to feel again the comforting embrace he'd given her that day a decade ago when her family's shop had burned to the ground.

Correction. The day *Hunter* had burned the workshop to the ground and destroyed Benton Woodworking, a livelihood the family had relied on for nearly a century. The day the police had arrested him for arson.

She recalled the savage blaze, how she'd

come home to find the family business overcome by heat so intense that all the firefighters could do was hose down her nearby home so it, too, wouldn't catch fire.

After all these years, the memory of those burning joists and beams still devastated her. A knot formed in her throat. *Dad, why didn't you have the strength to fight the cancer? I need you. I have no one now.*

A scene from three days ago flooded back. Rae hated the memory. Her dad, in the hospital, weakened and bone thin, had grabbed her hand with surprising strength and forced her to agree to the unthinkable. He'd asked her to forgive Hunter and let . . .

Robert Benton had collapsed, unable to finish his sentence.

To placate her father, she'd agreed. But forgive Hunter? *Never.*

All she wanted was to be left alone to mourn her dad's death, and to continue to build the business. And forget she ever knew Hunter Gordon.

The organist started playing some soft, sad music. Rae felt the touch of the funeral director's white-gloved hand and allowed him to direct her to her seat.

Sitting, she watched Hunter scan the crowd, his suspicious eyes probing each face. When he reached hers, he swung around to find a chair as far away as possible.

His presence, however, filled the chapel, overpowering the somber mood with an emotion Rae refused to analyze.

"Who's that?"

Rae looked into her cousin's red-rimmed eyes. Annie Dobson had spent the last three days crying. Rae appreciated the sentiment; after all, Dad had been Annie's favorite uncle. But with her own emotions roiling like oil and water, Rae could barely answer.

She finally forced the words through gritted teeth. "Hunter Gordon."

Annie's jaw dropped. On her other side, her husband swore. With his thick, dark brows knitted together, Kirk tried to locate Hunter in the crowd.

"Never mind him," Rae stated quietly.

"We can ask him to leave," Annie suggested.

"Or kick him out," Kirk muttered.

The ideas tempted her, but Rae shook her head. There had been no collective gasp of recognition, and she didn't want to make a scene. "Let him be. I don't care if he's here or not." Despite her words, she stole another glance around. Andy Morrison had just slipped in and was making his way to the only available chair — beside Hunter.

Quickly, Rae faced the front, not wanting Andy to catch her eye. Of course he'd come. Thinking himself her suitor, he'd find any excuse to be near her.

Hot tears stung her eyes during the service. Battling them turned her body into a tight bundle of quivering nerves. And the whole time, she felt Hunter's heated gaze fixed on her.

Perhaps she *should* ask the director to remove him. But she really didn't want to cause a scene at her father's funeral. Dad deserved better.

Rae dared another short glance over her shoulder. Hunter had matured in prison, into a handsome man who wore wariness as easily as she wore the loose navy suit Annie had loaned her for the funeral.

His nose looked as if it had been broken a few years back. On one side a scar ran from his nostril to the dark blond hair at his temple. His closed eyes and bowed head added a secrecy to his demeanor. Was he praying?

She snapped her attention to the front, where the pastor was finishing his short message.

What was Hunter praying for? Dad was dead, and Hunter had better not be praying for her to find peace. He had no right! she

13

thought with outrage.

A moment later, she felt contrition swooping in. That wasn't fair to Hunter.

After the casket was wheeled past, Rae let her cousin guide her out, keeping her head down to avoid the eyes of the crowd, and especially Hunter.

The interment half an hour later was pure torture. Autumn had provided a clear day with a warm wind, enticing well-meaning mourners to linger.

Relief washed over Rae when she and Annie entered the church hall, where refreshments waited. Hunter was nowhere in sight. If God had any mercy at all, she'd never see Hunter Gordon again.

"I believe Rae's in danger. We both are. You've got to help us, Hunter."

Recalling Robert Benton's last visit, just over a week ago, Hunter stopped at the edge of Rae's driveway. His mentor had shown him pictures of the new building.

Being here now felt so unreal. Hunter had been barely an adult when he'd gone to prison. Now he was nearly thirty.

One time, early on, when Benton had visited, he'd chided Hunter for fighting, saying it would lessen his chances at an early parole. Hunter hadn't wanted to see him

14

that day, let alone listen to a lecture.

Things had changed.

Today, Hunter smiled humorlessly into the thick woods beside the driveway. He'd ended up serving the full sentence. He'd survived the "range," a place where cells faced each other across what was dubbed one of the meanest streets in Canada.

More than survived. After establishing a mean reputation, he'd done a 180, and given his life to Christ.

The warm breeze snaking through Green Valley waned in this sheltered corner near the top of the hill, but it still carried dampness from the nearby Bay of Fundy. Why was he really here? He owed Benton nothing, a part of Hunter argued. He'd kept Benton's secrets, even when Benton wanted to ease his conscience and tell Rae everything.

Again, that last visit returned to him. "You have to keep Rae safe, Hunter. She's in danger. I don't trust anyone else."

He'd straightened. "Why? What's going on?"

"I don't have all the proof yet." The old man had swiped a shaking hand across his gaunt face. "It's complicated. I tried to tell you in a letter once, but it was too dangerous."

"More dangerous than what we'd been doing?"

Benton had nodded. Hunter had folded his arms, then unfolded them. *Help me forgive him, Lord.* "What's going on?"

"Someone's lurking around the shop. I found gas-soaked rags there. I burned them in the woodstove before I told Rae. She didn't believe me. We need to figure out what to do when I come get you. It's only a week away." The man had coughed violently, drawing the attention of other visitors in the room.

Hunter knew then that the cancer was really bad. His chest had tightened. "You should go back to your doctor."

"After I'm done here. But first, listen. I talked to God last night. I know He's forgiven me, but I feel I should tell Rae about the fire."

Hunter had shaken his head. "Do you think that's wise?" He'd leaned closer as clarity slammed into him with shocking force. "You'd have to tell her everything. It'd be too hard on her."

"She deserves the truth. I only just told her about the cancer."

"You only just told her? How is that possible? I mean, you knew before I was arrested."

Benton looked contrite. "I went into remission, and I didn't want to worry her. She'd fuss, and with the business not so good, we couldn't afford for me to start taking time off."

Was that all? Hunter could tell his old mentor was holding something back. Something about the business, or maybe something about their little scheme?

"I know I'm not doing things your way, Hunter. But she deserves the truth, whether or not I told her about the cancer."

Dread trickled through Hunter. "At least wait until I'm out. I'll go with you."

Benton's lip had quivered, and remorse ripped through Hunter. The old man was dying. For all of his faults, and his late coming to faith, did he need to die now?

At that very moment, the buzzer had sounded throughout the cafeteria, ending the visiting hour. Benton rose wearily, and Hunter caught his arm. "Wait! What about this danger? You should tell Rae *that.* Or at least tell the police."

The old man had shrugged off his hand. "Believe me, the police can't be trusted. I think I'm being followed. Look, you'll be home soon. We'll figure something out." He threw a hasty glance toward the door.

"You have to tell the police now!"

17

Benton hesitated. Finally, he nodded. "I will."

With that, he'd shuffled out, and Hunter hadn't seen him alive again. According to the gas station clerk, Robert Benton had collapsed at his doctor's office, and four days later, semiconscious and delirious, he'd died in hospital.

Now, staring at Rae's house, with the graceful birch trees behind it, Hunter felt a sense of loss. He had nowhere else to go. With no family, no job, only an old man's confused warning, he'd come here.

The growl of an engine caught his attention. He stepped from the driveway to the grass, in time to see Rae's truck screech to a stop in a cloud of dust. The driver's door swung open and she alighted swiftly. "Get off my land."

The welcome he'd expected. Hunter dropped the duffel bag he'd purchased from the prison stores in anticipation of his release, saving the pittance an inmate earned for that one item. In it was a change of clothes, a charity toiletries kit, his Bible and a small amount of cash.

"It's okay. I just came —"

He shut his mouth. She was mad at him. And if he were to try to warn her that her life was in danger, she wouldn't even listen to him. Besides, what would he say when she'd invariably ask why her father had visited him? Hunter would have to tell her everything.

Forget it. It wasn't his job to speak ill of the dead. And she sure wouldn't want *him* of all people, to talk to her. In *her* mind, he'd burned down her family's livelihood.

In front of him, Rae had planted her feet shoulder width apart and settled her hands on her hips. "You're not welcome here. You destroyed our lives ten years ago, and drove my father to an illness he couldn't fight. Now get off my land!"

He swallowed. Even in her anger and grief, Rae was a Beautiful woman, though she'd look better in a softer color to compliment the sun in her hair, he decided, rather than the harsh navy of her ill-fitting suit. "There isn't anything that would make you feel better, Rae. Still . . ." He faltered. "I just want to say how much your dad meant to me."

Her expression wavered. She blinked and the chin that had shown determination a moment ago now wobbled in a telltale way.

His heart wrenched. He took a step toward her, wanting to haul her close and comfort them both.

She jerked back. Then, snatching a Tupperware container from the bench seat, she slammed the truck door and stalked toward the house. "Leave. I don't want to see anyone, not for a long time."

He shrugged. "I've got nowhere to go. This was my only home."

When she bit her lip, he hated the guilt he was heaping on her. "The prison system doesn't turn people out into the cold, Hunter," she protested.

"True. There's a group home in Moncton, but that's seventy kilometers away." He was crazy to come here. To keep a woman who hated him safe from an unknown danger? Maybe Benton's mind had begun to deteriorate from the cancer, and he'd only imagined a threat.

Rae's eyes glistened in the late afternoon sun.

Guide me, Lord. Do You want me to help her?

She bit her lip, obviously grieving.

She had no one. Right then, he knew he couldn't leave Green Valley.

Some time ago, Rae's father had offhandedly told her that unless released inmates had family and friends, they were on their own.

Guilt flooded her, and she knew this was

what her pastor called the touch of the Holy Spirit. Her father's voice seemed to reach through the confusion. *"You must forgive him, Rae."*

The words added to the ache behind her eyes. Breaking her last promise to her father was something she wanted to do, yet couldn't.

With a halfhearted step toward Hunter, she heard herself say, "Why don't you come in? I've had a ton of food dropped off the last few days. You must want a home-cooked meal."

He had the most intense gaze, something she hadn't noticed a decade ago. And if she correctly judged the flare of interest there, he was hungry.

"Thanks."

Once inside, he glanced around curiously.

"Yes, it's all the same," she said, noticing his hesitance. "We didn't have time to remodel after you . . ." She stopped, slipping the plain black pumps off her hot, tired feet. "We put all the insurance money into the new workshop."

Hunter peered out the back window. "It looks good."

Well, that was one thing they agreed upon. The new workshop, sturdy and welcoming, stood as a monument to Robert Benton's hard work, despite the cancer.

He'd had that horrible disease for ages. She knew it had started its ravaging years before, despite him blaming various colds for his symptoms. Fresh tears stung her eyes. *Lord, why all this suffering? Dad loved You. Yes, it took him all this time to give his life to You, but . . .*

She grabbed the coffee tin. Thrusting it at Hunter, she muttered, "Can you make a pot? I have to change." She plucked at the navy skirt she wore. "I borrowed this from my cousin Annie. Do you remember her?"

"I met her when she came for your father's birthday party that time, and her husband sneaked beer into the house."

Rae walked into the hall. "Yes. Dad sent him home in a taxi."

Hunter's deep voice rolled across the kitchen. "No. I drove Kirk home."

"But Dad said . . ." Stopping in her tracks, she frowned. Ten and a half years was a long time ago. And shortly after that night, Hunter had lit a pile of gas-soaked rags in the shop. She'd forgotten all about the party until this very minute.

Wait. Hadn't Dad said something recently about gas-soaked rags? He'd looked deeply concerned, but she hadn't believed him.

With pursed lips, she stared across the

quiet kitchen at Hunter. He didn't move, not even to start the coffee she could really use. His eyes remained fixed on her, making heat rush to her face.

"No, your father didn't call a taxi, Rae. I drove Kirk home that day."

Indignation flared. Hunter had no right to correct her about her father, not on the day she'd laid him in the ground. Not when the very stress of what Hunter had done had killed him.

"Forget it, Rae. Go get changed." He turned his attention to the coffeepot, leaving her torn between the urge to tell him off or flee.

She pivoted and strode up to her bedroom.

Hot, restorative coffee bubbled and dripped, the soothing sounds and scents dancing up the stairs when she emerged from her bedroom a few minutes later. She found Hunter setting cream and sugar on the table beside the triangle sandwiches and sweet squares she'd brought home from the church hall. A pot on the stove told her he was warming the chicken soup a neighbor had dropped off yesterday.

"Did you have anything to eat after the funeral?"

"Yes," she lied.

He slanted her a look, taking in her jeans and cotton shirt. "The first thing a person learns in prison is that everyone lies. You get a lot of practice recognizing it."

This was ridiculous. There was nothing shameful in being hungry. She sank into a chair. Feeling like a starving animal lured out of its hole by food, she reached over to snatch a sandwich.

Hunter poured the coffee and then slid the cream and sugar her way. He took his black and hot, she noticed. Well, if he could, she could.

But after one sip of the strong, scalding brew, she reached for the cream. Then the sugar.

"The woodworking business is still good?" he asked.

"Good enough." She bit her lip at yet another lie.

His eyebrows shot up. Her grip on her mug tightened. "Why is that a surprise? Dad wasn't the only person who worked here. I liked carpentry before you . . ."

Then, seeing his tight jaw, she questioned the wisdom of letting him into her house. He was, after all, a felon.

"You did a good job," he said mildly. "Your father —"

Anger rose, unbidden. "What about my

father? What could you possibly say about him?"

"Nothing. That's why I shut up."

She couldn't stop, not after the day she'd had. "You have no right to say anything. I let you come in for a coffee and a bite to eat because you have nowhere to go."

She shut her eyes, wanting to grieve alone. Hunter's appearance had forced to the surface a deathbed promise she hadn't expected to fulfil, and wasn't sure she could.

"Being angry all the time will eat away at you, Rae. It's like violence. It solves nothing."

She peered at him. "And you with the broken nose should know this?"

"Along with the dislocated shoulder, twisted knee and a nasty scar from my chest to my neck. Yes, I know. Benton told me plenty of times I wouldn't get anywhere with violence or anger."

Rae felt her jaw sag slightly. Abruptly, Hunter stood. He helped himself to some soup. She twisted around. "When did my father tell you that?"

He didn't look at her. At least not right away. When he did, his expression was hooded. "From the moment he met me in Moncton, until the day . . ." Hunter drew in a long breath ". . . the day I set fire to the

25

workshop. Your father told me violence doesn't solve problems. It creates them."

Rae frowned. Hadn't he just told her everyone lies in prison? Surely that included him? Had Dad really said that to him, or was Hunter fabricating a story to prove she was wrong to accuse him?

Her heart tightened. She *was* wrong. Scriptural words echoed in her head. *Vengeance is mine. I will repay.* With as much dignity as she could muster, she took the mugs and dumped the lukewarm coffee down the sink. Then dared another glimpse at him. Hunter seemed unusually awkward.

She did not want to analyze why, especially when the phone on the wall beside her rang.

Five minutes later and quite bewildered, Rae hung up. Her father's lawyer, Mr. Le-Blanc, wanted to see her now, if possible.

Not just her. Mr. LeBlanc had requested Hunter come, too. Her stomach tightened with concern. Why? Because of Dad's will?

This was making for a long day. She'd seen Mr. LeBlanc briefly at the funeral, but he'd only had a chance to offer his condolences. While she could have begged off, she also knew she wouldn't be working today. She may as well get this necessary reading of the will over and done with.

She turned to Hunter. "That was Dad's

lawyer. He wants to see us as soon as possible."

Hunter's brows shot up. "Me, too?"

"Yes, you, too."

Rising, he covered the food. She tried to swallow to soothe her dry throat, but an uneasy feeling persisted. Something wasn't right.

"Rae! Come in!"

Rae looked up to see Mr. LeBlanc standing by an inner office in his house. She crossed the low-pile carpet toward him. Over her head, she heard the lawyer address Hunter.

"Mr. Gordon, I presume. It's good to get a hold of you two so quickly. Come in and sit down."

They followed him in. Hunter's expression turned wary as he accepted one of the leather chairs tucked around a table. A heavy man with more hair on his face than his head, the lawyer took a seat across from them and slipped on his reading glasses.

Rae fidgeted. Her father had mentioned briefly his will once, years ago. She'd heard nothing more. So why was Hunter needed? To be the executor?

"I appreciate you seeing me on short notice. Your father wanted his estate tidied

27

up as quickly as possible after his death. Though I'm sure he wasn't expecting it so soon." The lawyer wore a look of shared sorrow. She nodded, and the lawyer continued. "Your father came to see me about seven years ago, and we made up a rough draft of a will. He didn't sign it until a month ago."

A month ago? Around the time of the alleged gas-soaked rags? Rae frowned.

"Your father asked me to be the executor of his will. It's quite unusual, but I agreed, given the circumstances."

"Which were?" Rae asked.

Mr. LeBlanc looked uncomfortable. "My conversation with your father was private, Rae. I'm sorry." With that, he began to read a series of preliminary paragraphs, legal jargon about certificates and debts and the Family Law Act.

"Mr. LeBlanc," she interrupted, touching the table between them. "This legal stuff is over my head. Just read the part that affects us, please."

He set the papers down and peered at her over his reading glasses. "Basically, your father has left you all his personal belongings, listed here." He freed a sheet from the portfolio and turned it around to face them. "But the real estate, that being the house, workshop and all the land around it, is to be shared jointly between you two."

You two? Had she heard right? Rae's mouth fell open as she blinked. "Shared? That's impossible! Hunter hasn't seen my father in years. It doesn't make any sense!"

Mr. LeBlanc lifted his brows and shifted his cool stare to Hunter. Their gazes locked for a tense moment, until the lawyer turned to Rae again. "Your father wanted this, Rae. I know it's hard to believe, but these *are* his last wishes. If you like, you can contest this will. But it could take years to resolve, and the court could order you to sell the land and split the money."

Gripping the edge of the table, she pushed back her chair and stood. "Sell? Benton Woodworking has been in my family for a hundred years. Dad wanted it to stay in the family, no matter what." To sell off Dad's pride and joy would be heartless, as if she was . . . well, somehow killing him herself.

She sagged back in her seat. The very fact that her father had willed half of all he owned to Hunter Gordon proved he couldn't have cared that much for Benton Woodworking. *Should* she contest it? Could she even afford to?

Mr. LeBlanc spoke. "Rae, do you want to contest this will?"

Finally, she shook her head. With the

stroke of a pen, her father had condemned her to share everything she valued with the man who'd destroyed her life.

Two

Again, Mr. LeBlanc asked, "Do you want to contest the will?"

Hunter watched Rae. Guessing her thoughts was easy: *If only she had the money to buy him out.*

Her eyes lingered on her father's signature. Was she thinking of Benton's life insurance? There should be enough remaining after the funeral expenses to buy out Hunter's share of the estate. Then she would own it all.

The thought caused something to lurch within him. He'd have money and freedom. He could leave, go somewhere to start again.

What about Benton's warning?

She stood. "No, I won't contest it. Do all the necessary paperwork, please. There's no hurry. I know there will be things like income tax, and any liens to be sorted out."

Hunter rose in turn as she reached across the table to shake Mr. LeBlanc's hand.

"Call us when you have the papers ready,"

she said, and walked past them both, out of the office and into the brilliant fall sunshine. Hunter shook the lawyer's hand, then followed her out.

She said nothing all the way home. As soon as she'd parked the truck, she hurried into the workshop. A few minutes later, Hunter found her scribbling notes on a pad at the desk there. He hesitated. It had been nearly an hour since the lawyer had dropped his bomb, and Hunter still hadn't absorbed it all.

Rae looked up as he walked toward her desk. "I guess I can't tell you what to do, now that you own half of everything."

Stolen from Rae, a voice inside him whispered, *because you and Benton dabbled on the wrong side of the law before Benton panicked when another man — what was his name? — began to threaten him.*

Was that the danger Benton had mentioned? Hunter pulled up a chair and sat at the end of the desk. "Rae," he began, "we need to talk. I wasn't completely truthful with you earlier."

"How so?" She looked up from her writing.

"You asked when your father talked to me about violence, and I let you believe it was before I went to prison. I'm sorry. He did talk to me in prison, about violence and about something else. He visited with me in jail."

She set down her pen and seemed to freeze there, waiting for him to continue. He went on. "Your father told me that you're in danger."

Her gaze pinned him. "In danger? How so?"

Here came the difficult part. How was he supposed to warn her, yet not tell her everything? Though Benton had wanted to confess his crime to his daughter, Hunter had no desire to tarnish his mentor's memory. It didn't feel right. For all Benton's faults, he'd been a good father. And God knew that Hunter hadn't been perfect, either. Enough reason not to defame the man.

Hunter leaned forward. "He didn't go into detail, probably because he knew someone could be listening."

"Why would he be concerned by that?" she asked innocently.

"All I know is he warned me that both of you were in danger, and that I needed to make sure you were all right."

She bristled. "I'm as fine as I can be right now. Are you sure he wasn't just asking you to check in on me occasionally?"

"If I were to just drop by to see if you're all right, why give me half the estate, knowing that would make me stay?"

Her lips tightened. "There is no danger here."

He scrubbed his face. "There is. Your father found gas-soaked rags here once, and thought he saw someone lurking around."

She perked up. "That was only a few weeks ago. This is a woodworking shop. Sometimes we use solvents. He probably smelled them. And as for someone lurking around, this is an attractive area. I own — *we* own nearly half of this mountain. There's public property all around here and people are bound to accidentally cross onto our land."

"Your father wouldn't warn me for nothing." Even as he said that, Hunter wondered again if Benton's mind had been ravaged by the cancer. "This is serious, Rae. You're vulnerable right now, and your father was concerned enough to ask me to make sure that you're safe."

She waved her hand. "As you can see, I'm safe."

He pressed on. "We should contact the police. They can step up patrols in this area, check out who might be using the land around you." As the words left his mouth, he knew he was being hypocritical. Ten years ago, he and Benton had stolen valuable wood from government land.

No. Even though he'd gone to prison for arson — not theft — he'd learned his lesson.

Leaning back, Rae shook her head. "The police won't do anything. They're too busy."

"Just go to them, Rae, or I will."

Her brows shot up. "They won't believe you."

"Then listen to your father one last time."

Rae pursed her lips. "We need proof. Did Dad write anything down?"

He sighed. "No."

"And you want me to go to the police anyway?"

"Your father was more than just concerned. Your safety meant more to him than anything. That's why he asked me to help. If you ignore his warning now, it'll be as if he meant nothing to you."

She sat a moment in silence. Hunter prayed for her to listen to reason.

Finally, she shrugged. "All right. We'll go, but I honestly don't think they can or will do anything."

Rae didn't want to go to the police, but even more, she didn't want anyone to think her father's love meant nothing to her. She was gathering up the papers on the desk, readying them for filing, when a sudden noise made her lift her head.

Something black whisked past the small window of the workshop door, startling her.

"What's wrong?" Hunter asked.

"I just saw something outside."

They moved toward the front of the workshop, but Hunter cut her off at the lathe. "Let me go first."

Rae nodded. She was no fool. Hunter was big and brawny, and in regards to security, he was an asset to her shop.

Good grief, was she actually taking his warning seriously?

He threw open the door and stalked out. Rae followed.

The front of the place was empty. She'd seen the movement to the left, and hurried to the end of the building, stopping at the corner nearest her house, only a few feet away. Beyond, the forest stretched, its golden autumn leaves quivering in the breeze from the bay.

Years ago, Rae's mother had planted New Brunswick violets along this shady side of the house, but after the shop had been rebuilt and the land trampled by workers, all that remained was moss.

Rae glanced along the house. A woman stood there, dressed in black, a digital camera dangling from her left hand.

Rae caught Hunter's attention, flicked her head toward the stranger. He strode over. "May we help you?" he asked.

The woman turned. She looked familiar, but like so many slim, bottle blondes, she could have been anyone. Smiling, she picked her way over the soft moss toward them, yanking out one narrow heel when it sank into the ground. Rae noticed her spiked sandals, a strange choice of footwear for the season. They didn't quite complement the expensive-looking business suit. Some of her hair had escaped the loose roll she wore, but she didn't seem to care. Her makeup didn't soften the hard edge to her expression, either.

Rae bit her lip. She liked herself, and what she'd become over the years, but a part of her regretted not being more feminine, as this woman seemed to be.

"Rae Benton?" The blonde said her name as though she'd just recognized an old school friend. She hadn't. Rae knew all her old classmates, and this woman wasn't one of them.

"Is there something I can do for you?" Rae asked as Hunter shifted closer to her.

She didn't need him to protect her. This woman was hardly a threat. Yet as soon as she thought that, she recalled her father's concern about finding gas-soaked rags. A woman could do that as easily as a man.

"I'm Christine Stanton." The blonde thrust out a business card. Hunter took it before Rae could move.

She glanced down at the card before he pocketed it. Real estate agent? That's where she'd seen her before. The woman ran her own agency, and her face graced flyers, whole pages in newspapers and occasionally the sides of city buses.

"What can we do for you?" Rae asked.

"This is a wonderful piece of property!"

"It was a land grant to my great-grandfather."

"Good hardwood?"

Beside her, Rae felt Hunter stiffen. "Like everywhere else," he answered.

Still smiling, Christine walked past them. When she reached the driveway, she peered upward. Rae owned half of the highest mountain in the area.

No. She and Hunter owned it now. Not that one could call the slope a mountain. Once, years ago, Rae had flown out to British Columbia to see her mother's family. Those things out there were mountains.

This was just a large hill.

All the same, its rounded peak rose high above the workshop. Rae was about to tell Christine how much of the mountain she owned when she stopped. It was hardly this woman's business.

As if sensing Rae's suspicions, Hunter said, "You haven't told us why you're here."

"No. I'm sorry. I'm here, Ms. Benton, to see if you'd be willing to sell."

"Sell what?"

"The house, the workshop, the property." Christine lifted penciled brows and fluttered her hand. "Your father is gone, and what use is all this to you now?"

Heat tore across Rae's cheeks and she bit down hard. It took locking her knees and a fast prayer to keep her from chasing the woman to her car.

Lord, give me some patience.

"You're not from around here, are you, Ms. Stanton?" Hunter asked.

"I recently moved to Green Valley, but I can tell a prime piece of real estate when I see one."

Or an opportunity to take advantage of someone in mourning, Rae thought savagely. As soon as she did so, she regretted it.

Forgive me, Lord. She was to be *in* this

world, but not a *part* of it. That meant not thinking so callously.

Hunter spoke. "Are you aware that Rae just buried her father this morning?"

Christine put on an appropriate look of sympathy, but Rae wasn't convinced of its sincerity. "I did know," the woman said. "And allow me to offer my condolences. I should have done that sooner. But being financially secure at this difficult time can help to ease the burden that mourning places on us. Your father was wise not to sell before this. The market wasn't ripe like it is now."

Rae frowned. "Are you saying you approached my dad before he died?"

The woman flushed. "Uh, no, I didn't. I just assumed that he would have thought it at some time. But now, eco land is growing in value, and this would bring you a tidy sum. I can offer you —"

"I am not ready to slap up the For Sale sign yet, Ms. Stanton. I'm sorry you had to come all the way up here to hear that, but my business is growing and I have no inclination to sell."

"Not to mention that I am half owner of this land."

Rae had wanted to deliver that tidbit later, but Hunter's words struck where they

40

needed to. Christine's jaw fell.

"Half owner?" she echoed.

"That's right," Hunter answered. "Robert Benton, Rae's father, willed the land to both of us, along with the buildings and the business. So whenever you feel the need to discuss business, both of us need to be present. And I agree with Rae. There's no need to sell, especially not today."

Rae felt Hunter's gaze settle briefly on her. While she wanted to stand up to this real estate agent by herself, she was quite glad to hear his words.

Maybe when she got her insurance money, she'd push for him to sell to her, but for now, they stood in united opposition to this worldly agent.

Rae liked the solidarity.

But it was hypocritical to want Hunter around only while it was convenient.

"I didn't know." Christine's voice had dropped, as if she'd been expecting something totally different. A second later, her bright smile returned. Swinging her camera sassily, she added, "I'm the best agent in the area and can get you a great price for this place."

"We're not interested," Rae said flatly.

After a glance at Rae, Hunter studied the woman with suspicion. "Why do you think this land is so special? What did you call it? 'Eco' land?"

"Just like those ecotours of environmentally sensitive areas of the world, I see places like this as returning to the way they should be, so the land can be enjoyed in an ecologically minded way."

Rae found it a strain to stay polite. She'd done nothing to this land, so how could the woman insinuate otherwise? "Well, you have no worries there. My woods are going to stay this way for a very long time. We don't allow lumber to be harvested anymore, and we don't do anything to the forest. It's exactly the way God meant it to be."

"Well, like I said, money can provide the security you need. Give it some thought."

"Who do you think might want this land?" Hunter asked.

She smiled again, making Rae shiver unexpectedly. "I have a few people in mind. Perhaps I could evaluate your property for you. Free of charge, of course."

"No, thank you," Rae answered.

"Are you sure? Acreage around here is going fast."

The woman wasn't getting the message, Rae thought. But she had managed to pique her interest. "What land around here? I haven't seen any For Sale signs, and behind me is all provincially owned forest."

"Don't be fooled by the lack of signs. This area is ripe for development and I want *you* to benefit from it."

Wasn't she kind? Rae wanted to answer her own question, but by then the woman had drilled one of her thin stiletto heels into the soft edge of the driveway. With a yank, she pulled her sandal free and sashayed back to her little black coupe. When she turned at the end of the driveway, the car door showed her bold, smiling face along with her agency's logo.

"I can't believe what just happened." With a shake of her head, Rae returned to the workshop. Hunter still stood outside. Through the window, she could see his back. He turned, as if scanning the property.

Her heart lurched. Was he actually considering Christine's offer? Was he thinking of forcing her to sell this place?

Would he thwart her desire to make this shop viable again? Worry gnawed at her and she did her best to discard it. *Don't borrow trouble. You have enough on your plate today to deal with.*

She'd make this place work better than ever before. She had to. She'd bring the business back to its former strength, and no one was going to stop her.

"Let's go."

Rae frowned at Hunter, who'd walked in while she was deep in thought. "Where?"

"To the police. We agreed, and we'd have been there and back by now if it wasn't for that woman. She doesn't change anything here. We need to talk to the cops."

He was still concerned for her safety. That seemed to squash any suggestion that he wanted money out of their new arrangement. Otherwise he would have used the threat, along with this offer of Christine's, to force her to sell.

She reluctantly followed him outside. It was going to be a long day. Reaching the truck, she turned. The half-bare trees beyond her house rattled in the wind, like dry, bony skeletons.

The milled lumber at the edge of the yard snagged her eye, and she saw that what had been a neat pile two weeks ago was now leaning awkwardly, almost like a makeshift teepee. Had the wind pushed over the boards? Or had trespassers knocked the lumber off its supports on their way across her land?

Shivering, she stole a glance at Hunter as he climbed into the truck. It was probably hikers, nothing more, and not worth mentioning.

All the way into Green Valley, she wondered how he was going to convince the police that someone wanted to hurt her. A dead man's complaint of gas-soaked rags, burned up now, and the notion of trespassers, probably Christine and her staff checking out the place, were hardly worrisome.

That was as crazy as Rae sitting in the police station foyer with Hunter, waiting patiently for some officer to come out and listen to a supposed warning from her father.

Hunter had to be insane to think that the local cops would act on such weak evidence. They were going to think her dad had become deranged from the cancer.

Tears stung Rae's eyes. She was hurting her father's memory by coming here.

An officer entered the small foyer. The tall man glanced down at her, then his curious gaze settled on Hunter, who had risen when the security door opened.

The two men stared at each other. Immediately, Rae sensed tension between them. The officer stiffened, and Hunter's hand strayed to his shoulder, where the scar showing above his collar deepened in color.

The policeman turned to her. "My name's Mike Halloway. How can I help you two?"

Hunter answered. "This is Rae Benton.

45

We need to report a danger to her."

Rae rose. She didn't want to censor Hunter's words, but perhaps she could tell the police what Hunter had told her, without making her father look like a fool. "There could be a small amount of danger to my life."

Halloway crossed his arms. "What makes you think that?"

She paused. "My father told him when he was in jail."

"Prison. Hunter was in the federal prison, not the provincial jail."

He knew Hunter had been incarcerated? They were on a first name basis? Was that the reason for his obvious tension?

"Whatever," she told the officer. "The point is, my father believed my life was in danger, and asked Hunter to come back here to discover why that was."

"Your father didn't know?"

Her cheeks warmed. "No, he didn't. And he didn't tell *me* anything about it. He probably thought he could handle it, and was too proud to ask for my help."

"Was it like him to do that?"

She wasn't sure. She'd thought that her father had kept her informed on most, if not all, issues of importance, but he hadn't told her about his will. Or even about his cancer until the very end. Feeling foolish, she shrugged.

Hunter looked impatient. "Can we discuss this in your office?"

"If you like." Halloway led them into the small station, past some desks and into a row of cubicles that served as offices. He indicated for Rae to sit.

She'd never been in a police station before. She'd never even talked to an officer of the law before. And doing so now felt like a waste of everyone's time.

"So," Halloway began, pulling up another chair, while taking out a large notepad and pen. "What has happened to make you two think someone wants to harm you?"

Hunter repeated everything he'd said to her.

Halloway's pen hovered over the paper, while Rae studied his profile.

She'd seen the officer before, she decided, at the hospital, the day before her dad had died. Moncton General Hospital was a busy place. There were usually dozens of people in the entrance alone. But she remembered seeing this tall policeman there.

Strangely, that memory made the hair on her scalp tingle and a chill trickle down her neck.

Halloway glanced up at her, his pen still

poised above the blank paper. He met her startled gaze coolly and she found herself wondering what he was thinking. Maybe about how they were wasting his time?

Letting her exasperation flare, she stood. This was ridiculous. "Look, Hunter, we've reported it, such as it is. I don't think there's anything serious going on."

Hunter scowled. "You may not care, Rae, but this could be serious. You can't ignore it."

"Why? What could be such a threat up there?"

Halloway looked over at Hunter. "What do you think we can do about this?"

Rae bit her lip. Hunter cared enough to drag her down to the station. Yet this was so foolish, so unnecessary.

She threw her little knapsack over her shoulder, then waved her hand. "Look, if you're not going to do anything, we won't waste time here. I've got too much to do."

"Let me take down some information and we'll increase our patrols by your house. Would you like us to drop by periodically?"

No, she didn't want them to. She wanted to go home and rebuild her business, not look like a child afraid of imaginary threats.

But Hunter answered, "It wouldn't hurt. It's coming into hunting season and there's a lot of unused land behind her house."

Halloway paused. The only words written on the paper between them were, *"Rae Benton feels there is a threat to her safety."*

She watched Hunter's jaw tighten and again she felt the uneasiness swell between the two. Halloway shot her a calculating glance, and more shivers rippled down her spine.

When the report was finally finished, she hastily signed the bottom of it. And found herself anxious to be free of the uneasiness lingering in the cubicle.

THREE

Outside, the day was ending, and Rae had nearly reached her truck, which she'd parked around the corner from the station, when she heard her name being called.

She turned. Her cousin was hurrying down the street toward her. At their small truck, half a block away, stood Kirk, his arms folded as he leaned against the front bumper.

"Rae!" Annie gave her a warm hug. Years ago, after the fire, she had tried hard to be a mother figure to Rae, but young herself, and without children, she had ended up being more of an older sister.

Rae returned the hug, and then Annie shot a short, suspicious look at Hunter, who hung back. "Did I just see you coming out of the police station? Goodness, why?"

Rae swallowed, not wanting to lie to her cousin. "It was nothing, really. I'll tell you all about it later, when I return that skirt suit. I want to get it dry-cleaned first."

"Never mind that. You hardly wore it for any length of time, and I know money is tight."

How would she know that? Annie had sat in on several brief consultations about the funeral arrangements, but hadn't been there when Rae discussed billing details.

Over Annie's head, Rae glanced at Kirk, who was idly kicking at some dry leaves. He was being a bit antisocial, but considering his opinion of Hunter, of course he wouldn't walk over.

Her cousin was chattering on, and Rae realized that she'd missed the first part. ". . . put you on the prayer chain. For peace and guidance?"

Did anyone really know what it was like to lose both parents? How hard it was to know that they'd never see any grand-children, be there for the good and bad that would inevitably happen? Her heart tightened as she refocused on her cousin. "Thank you. That sounds nice."

Annie threw one more glance at Hunter, before guiding her away from her truck and him. "Are you okay? I mean, what is he doing here with you?"

Steeling herself, Rae answered, "Dad's lawyer called me shortly after the funeral.

He read Dad's will to me."

"What did it say?"

"Dad gave half of everything to Hunter."

Annie gasped. "That's crazy! You have to fight this, Rae. It isn't right."

"It's what Dad wanted. I have to respect that."

Annie quickly glanced over at her husband, who, although still lingering some distance away, had grown interested in their conversation. "Your father was sick, and maybe that was affecting his judgment. You can tell the judge that and get him to overturn the will. You deserve that land."

Behind her, Rae felt Hunter close in. Once again, she was glad for it. Annie meant well, but she was wrong here. Rae had to respect her father's decision.

Odd, though. Annie had thought the world of her uncle, and been ecstatic when he'd given his life to the Lord. She had even quoted the Biblical story of the laborers who all got paid the same despite how much time they'd put in. It had been a comfort to Rae after Dad had been admitted to the hospital.

But to now condemn his decision? It was very odd indeed.

"Annie, it's just something we have to get used to. Hunter is going to be around for a while." She decided not to say anything about her hopes of buying him out, at least not yet.

Her cousin leaned close. "Just be careful, Rae. And how are you, financially? Do you have enough money? I could lend you some. Just between us."

Did she mean not to tell Kirk, or Hunter? It was obvious Annie didn't trust Hunter, but Kirk had often complained she spent too much money.

Rae shook her head. "I'm going to call Dad's life insurance company soon, and get that matter settled. I'll come over with the suit as soon as I can. We'll have a nice talk over a hot cup of tea."

Annie began to turn toward her husband, but stopped. "Come during the day. Kirk will be at his shop." She leaned in for another hug, and added quietly, "Be careful. Hunter is a criminal, however kind he acts."

"I saw him praying at the funeral." Even as she murmured the words, she wondered at the sudden need to defend him. Was it because he'd stood up with her against Christine Stanton? Or was it perhaps the concern in his warning? Confusion swirled as she remembered the fire he'd set ten years ago.

She should hate him.

And yet, her father had given *his* life to the Lord. Had Hunter also?

She found herself whispering, "I think he's a Christian."

" 'Not everyone who says to me, Lord, Lord, will enter the Kingdom,' " Annie quoted softly before pulling away.

Rae watched the Dobsons drive off, lifting her hand to wave. As Kirk did a U-turn in the middle of the quiet Green Valley street, Rae wondered why they'd been down this way. They lived up by the highway, and his electrical repair shop was near a stretch of abandoned buildings nearby. Coming down here was as odd as Annie's quote from the Gospel of Matthew. Always a staunch Christian, Annie had sounded strange, issuing a warning as she had.

With a sigh, Rae turned and climbed into the truck. As she started the motor, she glanced toward Hunter. "Annie's always looking out for me. Dad was her favorite uncle."

"But she doesn't trust me."

"Don't take it personally," Rae answered, knowing that he would. "It's going to take time."

"For you, too?"

She thought again of her father's life

insurance, and felt a wave of hypocrisy. Instead of answering, she yanked at the gearshift and pulled out of the parking space.

Hunter couldn't stop staring at the land around him as he climbed out of the truck. Being incarcerated so young, he'd never owned property. Now he co-owned a piece so huge it already had vultures circling.

Benton's desperate warning came back to him, the fruitless visit to the police adding to its sharpness. The old man had been serious, and now Hunter had to be, as well.

The workshop phone rang, its outside buzzer piercing the air like a fire bell. Rae scrambled to unlock the shop door, then hurried over to the desk.

Within a minute, it was obvious the caller was a client with whom her father had a large contract. Three weeks ago, Benton had told Hunter about it. It had been the first big order in months, a project that would restore life to their sagging business. When Robert's health had taken a turn for the worse, most contracts had followed suit.

Hunter tightened his lips. Now Rae had the unpleasant task of telling the news about her dad. Even at this distance, he could hear the man's voice. The client was shocked, contrite . . . but concerned about his own deadline.

Gripping the receiver, Rae threw a plaintive look across the room at Hunter. She didn't possess the extra hands to complete the order in time.

Hunter strode across the shop, gently pried the phone from her grasp and spoke into it. "When did you need the first shipment by?" he asked after a brief conversation. Rae's head jerked up, her eyes wide. Shortly after, he ended the call.

"I can't fill that order, you realize," she said.

"Yes, you can," he answered.

She looked tired and worn. "How? I need Dad's skill, and he had all the paperwork, made all the arrangements —"

"Your father had the information. That guy said it's all in a file here. I know exactly what he needs."

Rising, she shook her head. "Dad promised a type of rare wood for the guy's banister spindles that I can't get!"

Hunter frowned. Benton had promised rare wood? Was it possible he was still involved with illegally harvesting timber? Hunter darted a glance at Rae, but she didn't seem to notice his hesitation.

"Besides, it's too much work for one

carpenter. Who's going to help me?"

He would have to. If Benton had been still stealing trees, which was becoming dangerously lucrative, that could be the reason for the danger to Rae. Hunter looked at her again. "I'll help."

"You? What do you know about woodworking?"

"I was your dad's apprentice for three years."

She blinked. "Ten years ago!"

He answered coolly, "I got plenty of on-the-job training."

She folded her arms. Irritated, he yanked the phone from its cradle and thrust it toward her. "Go ahead, call that guy back. Tell him you can't fill his order. And don't forget to add that you'll be lining up at the food bank for groceries by the end of the year, because if you don't fill this contract, you'll starve this winter."

She looked shocked. "How do you know I need money?"

"If you had any money or credit, you'd have offered to buy me out right there in the lawyer's office." He tilted his head, his expression quickly turning sympathetic. "Rae, we can do this. Give me a chance."

The set of her mouth revealed doubt. "There's some intricate detail work in this order, Hunter."

He hung up the phone, drawing on his reserves of patience. "I haven't been making pine coffins, Rae. I *can* help you. If we run into a snag, we can subcontract."

With her thumb and forefinger, she rubbed her forehead. "Dad knew where to get the rare wood, but I don't. There are too many details to work out. I can't do it."

And, Hunter added silently, seeing the turmoil in her face, *there are way too many emotions and memories tangled up in this workshop for you to tackle a contract right now.*

But Benton Woodworking had made a commitment.

He walked closer, then pressed his hand on the desk, inches from hers. His voice dropped to a soft murmur. "Let me help you, Rae. This is half my business now, and I want it to succeed as much as you do."

He had to help. If Benton had been doing something that might endanger his daughter, Hunter needed to be here.

Finally, she nodded. "It's not going to be easy."

He didn't back away, but rather, leaned forward. "I've lived for the last decade on the meanest streets in Canada."

She shook her head. "You've been in

prison for the last ten years."

He smiled grimly. "That's what some guards call them. Cops patrol the regular streets, but guards have to patrol the meanest streets. I survived them and I'll survive this. Besides, I have the greatest Ally a sinner could ever hope for."

She shot him a confused frown, obviously doubting his sincerity. It didn't matter to him. Hunter knew the truth in his heart, and he'd faced disbelief before.

Still, it wasn't hard to figure out the argument roiling within her. Hunter was an ex-con, and he'd told her that everyone in prison lies.

He cleared his throat. "I know it's hard to trust me right now, but that's what I'm asking. Will you?"

She paused. "If you think you can do it . . ." Pushing away from the desk, and him, Rae stood. "But if you don't mind, it's late. And too much has gone on today. Can we start again in the morning?"

He straightened. As soon as the words left her mouth, he knew what they meant. She wanted him to leave.

Except he had nowhere to go.

As if just realizing that, she turned. "Sorry. I forgot you don't have a place to stay." She cleared her throat. "Out back is a small annex. Over the years, Dad puttered at fixing it up. It has a bed and bathroom and a kitchenette. Dad said if I ever got married, he'd move in there and give me the house. You can stay there. But I'm warning you, it's small."

Was she implying it was too small for a newly released prisoner? Was she letting him stay there until he figured he deserved a bigger place, now that he was free?

"Thank you." He peered out the small workshop window. Already, the sun had slipped below the horizon, the world preparing for another long night. "Go to bed, Rae. Get a good night's sleep."

As he swung around to head out the door, she stopped him and handed him her house key. "Wait! Take some of the food from the refrigerator in the house. I won't be able to eat it all, and I know you haven't eaten much all day. Just leave the key on the kitchen table. I'll be right in."

He nodded and walked out of the workshop. In the kitchen, he carefully took only enough to hold him until he got groceries. The rest of the food was meant for Rae. And she'd need it.

He shut the fridge. Then, on an afterthought, he cruised through the house, checking locks and windows, anything that might threaten her. Satisfied, and not wanting to intercept Rae, he quickly left. She'd had enough of him for one day.

Inside the annex, Hunter set the food on the bed. While being infinitely better than a cell, the annex *was* small. A man could get claustrophobic if he didn't have experience dealing with small spaces.

Before the evening air could chill the room, Hunter shut the door. To his left, under the window, stood a small fridge and a two-burner propane cooktop, with a tiny sink and cupboard. Between all that and the bathroom was a chest of drawers. On top sat a small television.

He opened the tiny fridge to set the food inside, and spied a thick T-bone steak through the plastic door to the freezer. Catching sight of his name, he grabbed the note taped to it.

Hunter, welcome home. Take care of Rae. Remember what we talked about. Don't let them trick her.

The note was signed "R.B."

Hunter sank onto the bed. If Benton had collapsed at the doctor's office the day he'd visited Hunter in prison, he must have bought this before, hoping to explain everything on the way home.

Too late now. The flimsy clues penned here weren't much help. What were the threats? Who were the people hoping to trick Rae?

Still frowning, Hunter looked around. This small room had been built for him, and having been backed into a corner by her father's will, Rae had let him use it.

With gritted teeth, he unpacked the few things he owned. Then, with a silent prayer of thanks, he grabbed the steak, plus a pan he found in the cupboard, and fired up the stovetop.

He didn't remember ever eating a decent steak like this one. While it cooked, he reached for a date square, thankful that Rae had noticed he was hungry. But it just hadn't seemed right to eat the food delivered to *her* by well-meaning mourners.

Still, the snacks and the steak were long gone by the time he crashed on the bed.

He was still asleep, Rae noted. He hadn't heard her soft knock, or the door open when she twisted the knob a minute later. The draft of cool morning air that rolled in hadn't disturbed him, either.

"Hunter!" she whispered as she peeked in.

The guy slept like the dead. Rae didn't want to step into the small room, but they had work to do. A quick glance around showed he'd settled it. Her father had taken her grandmother's quilt for the bed, plus warm fleece sheets. Her inspection returned to Hunter's face. This was his first full day of freedom. She shouldn't deny him one sleep-in.

With a feeling of guilt, she noted the small garbage can holding the remains of a steak and its wrapper and tray.

Plus a note with Hunter's name on it, in her father's handwriting, though the words were smeared.

Dad had bought Hunter a steak? They could barely afford groceries right now, and her father had purchased a top quality, twenty-dollar steak?

Irritation rolled over her. Here she'd risen early, eaten leftovers and prepared for a day that would begin her healing and earn some much-needed money, while Hunter, full of steak, slept in. . . .

Louder than before, she called his name for a third time.

When he still didn't move, she knew something was dangerously wrong.

FOUR

"Hunter!"

His eyes shot open. "What's wrong?"

Rae blew out a sigh. "I couldn't wake you. It's time to get up. We have work to do."

He closed his eyes, looking pained. "In a minute."

Sympathy washed over her as he lay there. He wasn't sick. He was just tired, something she felt herself.

Embarrassed by the sudden intimacy, she backed away, bumping into the door.

He opened his eyes again, giving her a full measure of the cobalt blue of his irises. "Wait! What's that scent you wear? You had it on yesterday."

She hesitated, surprised by his question. "There's no point wearing perfume when I spend all day in a workshop. It's just a lotion."

"What's it scented with?"

"Roses." She shrugged self-consciously.

64

"I . . . I like it."

"I can see why. It's soft. A good choice for you."

She cleared her throat. This conversation was becoming a little too personal. She reached behind her to grab the knob of the still-open door. "Why do you ask?"

The pained frown returned. "I once knew someone who wore a scent like that."

"Your mother?"

"Hardly. She smelled like cigarette smoke. No, it was my first foster mother."

"First?" Rae knew Hunter had spent time in a foster home, but more than one? "Why didn't you stay with her?"

"She and her husband were killed in a domestic dispute with another foster kid's parents." He shifted, as if hoping to terminate the conversation.

Rae bit her lip. "I'm sorry. I'll leave you to get up, then. Meet me in the workshop." She made a hasty exit, finding herself pulling the cool morning air into her lungs as she headed into the shop. Then she straightened. Her father had bought Hunter a steak. He'd built that annex with him in mind, even written him a welcome note, hoping Hunter would help him find a threat, as if only he could do that. Why?

For that matter, why had Dad given him

65

half of the estate? As incentive for him to stay? Walking toward her desk, Rae thrust aside her questions. She didn't have the time or the energy to waste on them. Dad was gone — oh, how it hurt to admit that — and she had things to do. She sat down and stared at the paperwork in front of her.

Then she remembered the call she'd made early this morning. Dad's insurance broker had been kind enough to squeeze her in today at noon, promising he'd have everything ready for her. She'd settle the life insurance policy and hopefully, in a few days, be able to offer Hunter a fair price for his half. Her disquieting feelings would leave with him.

Encouraged by that thought, she picked up a note her father had put in the contracts file. The door to the workshop opened and she stiffened her spine. On the threshold stood Hunter, silhouetted against the bright morning light. He'd grown into a husky, powerful man, but today he looked tired, his shoulders hunched and his head lowered as he reached to rub his right temple.

She stood, unable to deny her growing sympathy. "You want some coffee? Dad keeps — kept — a pot and a small fridge here." Without waiting, she walked behind the desk to the pint-size refrigerator, upon which stood a coffee machine and some cups. She quickly set about brewing a pot, finding she needed a strong cup herself. When Hunter approached, she threw him a glance over her shoulder.

He looked worse close up. What had he indulged in last night, besides the steak, on his first night of freedom?

"You look awful. What'd you have? A one-man party last evening?"

He shot her a cool look. "The only thing I did was eat a steak, which was very good, then those desserts you gave me. I don't drink, smoke or do any sort of drugs."

"So all you did was eat and sleep?"

"And read my Bible. The prison chaplain gave me a study guide to Job, and I was doing that before I was released, so I continued."

The memory of the funeral, and of seeing Hunter offer up a prayer, returned. She didn't want to hear how he had found God, asked for forgiveness, and — as much as she didn't like the truth right now — been forgiven.

He grabbed a mug and poured coffee from the pot before it had even stopped dripping. The steaming liquid sizzled onto the burner underneath. He took a sip from his mug and winced slightly.

Rae blew out a sigh. "You've picked up a bug."

"I'll be fine in a minute."

"Maybe it was too much steak." As she spoke, she wondered if maybe she *did* resent her father giving him that steak.

Forget it. She bustled back to the desk. "Are you ready to work? Because I need you to find some things."

Her words were clipped, reminding him of the way he'd been treated in prison. No one really cared about him. . . .

Hunter drained his coffee and ignored the headache stabbing at him. "What's first?"

He took the short list of supplies she handed him. "I assume that the shed out back holds a bunch of stuff."

"Yes, but Dad had supplies everywhere. I need to make a few phone calls before we go into the city. Hopefully by then you'll know what we need to pick up." She pulled out the phone book from under a messy stack of papers. The resulting draft wafted that soft scent of roses over to him.

Hunter automatically inhaled, then stopped himself. He was here to protect Rae. From what, he didn't know yet, but he'd never find out sucking in rose-scented air.

He stifled a yawn. In the middle of the night, he'd awoken, and unable to sleep, he rose. He'd searched the workshop for several hours, looking for some clue as to who would want to harm Rae. By four o'clock, he'd found nothing.

He pivoted on the heel of his boot now and strode outside. He'd just have to keep his eyes open.

The hours ticked by and the headache eased only slightly. He spent the morning assembling the lumber needed for the job, and finding to his irritation that Benton had become disorganized over the years.

Living in a small cell had taught Hunter to be rigid with his own sense of order. More than once, his discipline came in conflict with other prisoners, and he had needed to defend himself. . . .

Enough. He wasn't there anymore. He was here, trying to rebuild his life, and help Rae. *Keep her safe.*

Lifting a pile of short boards and a drop cloth near the desk, he peered down at a large leather punching bag. Beside it, sealed in clear plastic, were a pair of boxing gloves.

His hand stilled as he reached for them. The medium-size box that held them was made from bird's-eye maple, cut and joined in Benton's unique grooved style.

The only source of that rare wood was on the government land behind their property. Was the illegal harvesting of wood they'd done a decade ago still going on?

Hunter lifted the gloves. "Were you planning on taking up boxing?"

"No. That was given to us a few weeks ago. The client couldn't pay us because he'd hit bottom, financially. I just couldn't make his life worse."

"So he gave you a punching bag?"

Shrugging, she returned to her work. Even with her head bent he could see embarrassment stain her cheeks. "He had nothing else."

"But it can't pay your bills."

Conceding, she flicked up a hand. "I can't take him to court. He's paying child support. I should try to sell the set." She peered over at Hunter. "Or you could use it."

Benton's firm words on fighting returned to him. "Punching a bag builds up a need to fight. It's better to learn to manage anger," he murmured.

"You don't look like you've stayed a pacifist."

"I won't fight." He dropped the boards back over the punching bag and gloves. Hunter knew she'd seen some of his scars, even though he'd worn a T-shirt to bed. If she continued to stare at him now, he didn't know what he'd do.

Eventually, he turned. "We have everything for the project, except, of course, the bird's-eye maple." He stepped in front of the box containing the gloves and bag, hoping she hadn't paid any attention to it. If she noticed the wood, with its distinctive swirls, she'd start asking questions.

"Fortunately, I found a lead on that," she answered. "But first, I have to head into town." She grabbed her knapsack purse. "I want you to come with me."

He had planned to, but the way she spoke made something in him go cold.

"Why?" Knowing the answer, he felt his jaw tightening. "Because you think I'll set fire to this place after you leave?"

She'd pressed her lips together, and he watched the pink spread up her neck to her face. "Surely you need to get things? Driver's license, banking details."

Yes, he did, but her smokescreen wasn't working.

Regardless of the surge of indignation, he recalled that fateful day a decade ago. Benton had sent Rae to her cousin's house, and instructed Hunter to drop the truck off at the service station.

But the truck had worked fine. Suspicious,

Hunter had circled back, returning in time to see the workshop engulfed in flames.

Later that day, the police found gasoline and some wood chips and rags in the truck cab. Benton told them Hunter had been complaining about the poor pay and demanding schedule.

His mentor had framed him.

Now, Hunter leveled his stare on Benton's daughter. "That was ten years ago, Rae."

Her cheeks reddening further, she returned his hard stare. "All I want is for you to do what you need to do while I'm in the city." She threw open the door. "It'll save time."

He couldn't refute her logic. *Let it go,* he told himself a minute later as they skirted the village of Green Valley on their way to Moncton. Once they were on the main highway Hunter watched the colors of autumn fly past. A small tan car had followed them up the on-ramp, and made Hunter suspicious. The radio announcer mentioned a tropical storm skirting the coast toward New Brunswick, and a heavy rainfall warning.

All the while Hunter battled the urge to spit out the truth to her, once and for all. Instead, clenching his jaw, he told himself again that Rae needed good memories of her father.

She adjusted the heat in the car. Though it was warmer today, heavy clouds covered the sky, matching his concern.

"What do you need to do?" he asked as they entered the city.

"I'm meeting with the insurance company."

The tall insurance building downtown had limited parking, but Rae found a space out back. Beyond lay the muddy and marshy Petitcodiac River, and past that, the sister city of Riverview, through which they'd passed. Everything had expanded so much in the last decade.

He undid his seat belt. "Am I allowed to come in, too?"

She climbed out. Her eyes glistened, and he could see that she was fighting her emotions. "I'm sorry you feel put out, Hunter, but it's going to take time to earn my trust again. I know it's not very Christlike, but it's the way I feel."

Well, at least she'd admitted it. But he'd paid a debt to society for a crime he hadn't committed, and he was working hard on forgiving Benton for all he'd done to him.

He was also working hard at safeguarding Benton's reputation. What Benton had done was wrong, but he'd been the only decent father figure Hunter had ever known. He'd been a good dad to Rae. Then the cancer had come, and Hunter had known he could never allow Benton to die in prison, alone. After that, covering for Benton started to snowball. He'd thought it was easier to keep Rae's memory of her father unsullied rather than hurt her with all the illegal stuff they'd done.

But could he have been wrong?

Hunter gripped the top edge of the truck box. He'd wanted her trust before he told her the truth, but maybe the trust would come *after* he told it.

The whole ugly truth.

FIVE

"Rae, there's something I —"

She didn't want to hear Hunter's thoughts. "I have to hurry —"

"Rae!"

She spun around at the new interruption. Striding toward her from his small, beige Saturn was Andy Morrison. She'd met Andy a few years ago, and since then, he'd shown up occasionally to ask her out. She'd declined, not being comfortable dating a man who didn't share her faith. The last time Andy had approached her, Dad had lost considerable weight. He'd attributed it to a flu virus. Weeks later, she'd learned finally about the cancer.

Andy stopped at the rear of the truck, shooting a curious glance at Hunter before focusing his attention on her. "What brings you into the city, Rae?"

"The life insurance company is ready to settle my father's policy."

His bland expression brightened for a moment. "I see." After another look at Hunter, he led her away from the truck. "I've missed you. I didn't get a chance to talk to you at the funeral, but you've been on my mind ever since."

Why was everyone ushering her away from Hunter? "The funeral was only yesterday, Andy."

"Yes, but life goes on, doesn't it?" He rubbed her elbow with his fingers, and she politely disconnected it from his grasp. "I'd like to drop by sometime, Rae. I care about you."

From the corner of her eye, she saw Hunter closing in. "Thank you, but I'm late."

Jealousy marred his even features. He flicked his head toward Hunter. "Are you seeing him? He didn't sit with you at the funeral."

Before Rae could answer, Hunter extended his hand. "I'm Hunter Gordon."

"Andy Morrison." The two men shook hands. "A *friend* of Rae's."

Rae rolled her eyes. Yeah, that would impress Hunter.

"I see," Hunter said. "So, you work in town?"

"Across the street. I just stepped out to

grab some lunch."

Hunter lifted his brows as he read the sign on the front of the building. It was a government office for land registration. As far as Rae knew, Andy was the financial officer in charge of registering deeds.

Hunter turned to him. "So you deal with government land?"

"Crown land," he corrected. "I control the leasing and purchasing of crown land." Andy's eyes narrowed. "Hunter Gordon, you say?"

"That's right. Hunter Ian Gordon, lately of Dorchester." Rae's words were clipped.

Andy frowned. Rae knew he understood that didn't mean the quaint village surrounding the infamous penitentiary, though both had the same name. He straightened. "It's nice to meet you, Mr. Gordon, but I don't expect we'll see each other again. Rae is busy and I plan to help her with all the details of running her workshop."

She shook her head. Andy knew nothing about her job, nor had she asked for help. His saber rattling needed to stop. "Andy, Hunter is half owner of the workshop. And thank you, but we don't need any help with the business." With that, she walked into the tall office building.

Rae was waiting impatiently for the elevator when Hunter strode up beside her. He said nothing about her comment to Andy, so she muttered. "I hope this isn't going to be difficult for you, Hunter, but my friends are bound to find out about you."

"That guy is no friend."

The elevator doors glided open and several people disembarked. She stepped inside, ahead of Hunter, and poked the fourth floor button. "Andy's been asking me out for months. He's persistent, if nothing else."

"What was your reason for not dating him?"

"He's not a Christian, and I feel that I should date only Christian men. Besides, Dad was getting sicker, and I was running the shop. I didn't have time."

"He's after something. And he's lying."

"You got all that from a twenty-second conversation on where he worked?"

"Morrison can't be trusted."

"And you know that because . . . ?"

"Because I've spent the last ten years with people just like Morrison, only *they* got caught."

"Of course you're going to think the worst. That's all you know."

But as soon as the words escaped her lips, she regretted them.

■ ■ ■ ■

She was right, Hunter conceded. It *was* all he knew.

His voice quiet, he asked, "I guess that means that you consider me the same?"

"Don't be so sensitive." Rae stared at the elevator door ahead of her, blinking several times. When it slid open, she walked out, straight to the receptionist.

He hung back. *Benton, what was the danger you couldn't tell me about? To help her, I may have to tell her everything. I'd be rubbing salt in her wounds.*

Once, during a fight five years ago, two lifers had pinned Hunter down. A third had taken a homemade knife — a shank — and sliced a line across his face in retaliation for Hunter saving the life of a visiting police officer the week before.

That officer had been Mike Halloway.

The inmate then yanked Hunter's head back and poured a mixture of salt and vinegar into his bleeding wound.

He could still feel the excruciating burn.

Today was much the same, he decided, as he followed Rae to the waiting area. He'd almost given in to the urge to tell her the truth. If Morrison hadn't arrived at just the right time . . .

I need to keep Rae safe, Lord. It's too much of a coincidence that Andy works for the government regarding the very land we were stealing trees from.

Twelve years ago, Benton had suggested cutting down certain rare trees from the adjacent public land — bird's-eye maple, curly maple. Though the unique qualities were hard to detect while the trees were still standing, Benton knew someone with a way of determining which they were. No one would miss them, he'd reasoned, and once the lumber was milled, no one would be able to trace it. It would be a lucrative, short-term operation, safe for everyone.

And now the man who controlled the leases on that land was interested in Rae?

Hunter leaned forward in his seat. "Morrison followed us into Moncton."

Before she could answer, an office door beside them opened and an older man walked out. He asked Rae to come in.

"I'll be a while," she told Hunter.

He grimaced at the interruption. "Take your time. I'll update my driver's license and my bank account."

After reinstating his driver's license, Hunter found his old bank, the same one Benton had used because Green Valley was too small for its own bank branch. Then found himself gaping at the teller in front of him.

Hunter shook his head and handed back his updated bankbook. "There's got to be some mistake, ma'am. The account should have only a few hundred dollars."

"Regular deposits were made, sir."

The staff at the penitentiary could deposit money for him, and had done so with the pittance of a salary he'd earned in the woodworking shop. But the balance shouldn't have been anywhere near this much. "Are you sure this is correct?"

The teller, an older woman, slid off her chair. "Let me dig out the deposit slips we still have."

She disappeared into a back office. When she returned, she spread out a handful of them. "They're all for the same amount, from the same depositor. Only the dates differ."

Hunter stared at the initials: *R. B.*

His heart tightened. Benton had slowly built up his bank account over the last decade, leaving Hunter with enough money to start over. To rebuild his life and put the past away forever.

Or to purchase Benton Woodworking in full.

Had the old man given him this money as payment for going to prison for him? Or for Hunter's silence? Or for the promise to look out for Rae after he died?

Hunter gritted his teeth. Maybe the last two, but there wasn't enough money in the world to compensate for a decade of his life and a criminal record.

Let it go. *Lord, help me forgive him.*

He looked at the teller. "This is an incredible amount. Why wasn't it investigated?"

His cellmate had laundered thousands. He'd told Hunter banks had major fraud departments, and tellers could easily report suspicious monetary transfers.

The woman gazed squarely at Hunter. "We investigate everything suspicious, but much of that is at a teller's discretion. It's a matter of knowing your clients. I knew Robert. I knew where the money came from. I didn't approve of what he was doing back then, and I still don't, but it was his choice to make."

The frost in her voice chilled Hunter. Was she referring to the illegal harvesting and selling of wood from public land? It was a real problem here in this province, and growing every year.

"Is there anything else you need, Mr. Gordon?" The woman's tone indicated she wanted their conversation to end.

Keep the money. Start again.

Gritty resolution scraped his insides, as if he'd eaten gravel. "Yes. There's one more thing I want to do."

Six

Where was Hunter? He hadn't been waiting for her when she'd emerged — in shock — from the office. And he wasn't at the truck.

The minutes dragged as Rae, biting her lip to stop from crying, peered toward the downtown district, then the mall. The throngs of people included no tall man with dark blond hair.

The visit to the insurance agency had hit her hard. She'd told the funeral director that her father had a life insurance policy and the bill would be paid. The check in her wallet wasn't enough to cover a tenth of the funeral expenses.

Now she faced another mountainous debt.

The fall breeze rolling down Main Street turned colder. With a shiver, and one last glance up the street, she finally spotted Hunter among the strolling office workers.

Relief sluiced through her, but she squelched the emotion before it took over.

Instead, she squared her shoulders as Hunter approached, knowing he would easily read her expression.

He seemed on guard himself. "Where have you been?" she asked when he reached her.

"I updated my bank account and renewed my driver's license." He looked grim. "How did it go for you?"

Bad. Worse than bad, when my father drained his life insurance policy over the course of several years. To do what? She had no idea.

She pivoted sharply. "I don't want to talk right now. Let's go. As soon as we get back, we have to start on that order. I've got bills to pay."

Hunter's brows lifted slightly, but he remained silent as they walked to her truck. Obviously, he'd learned in prison the enviable art of keeping quiet.

Concern weighed heavily on her, even at the bank, when she deposited the check and once again withdrew from the business's line of credit. At that moment, all she wanted to do was sag against the Instant Teller.

Later, in the workshop, she dug around for the note she'd found earlier. Her father had scrawled out a phone number for

Cutter Stevenson, the supposed source for the wood she needed.

Hunter came to stand beside her. "Let me call."

Outside, a branch that had grown too long during the summer scraped a harsh rhythm on the metal roof. The wind picked up as did the telltale heaviness before a rain rolled in again.

"No, thanks. This is my job."

You should be grateful for his help, a voice inside her stated. She grabbed the phone and dialed before all her remaining strength drained away.

After scribbling down directions to Cutter's place, she hung up. Another difficult call over and done with. The man had heard of her father's death, and offered another round of condolences she couldn't stand to hear.

"Do you know this guy?"

She gripped the paper. "No, which is surprising, considering he knows my father."

Hunter scanned the instructions. "His place is on the other side of the park."

"Yes." Fundy National Park was a sprawling reserve to the west, and the directions would lead her deep into the back roads beyond that.

"We're supposed to get that tropical storm

this evening," he said. "We should at least wait until tomorrow."

"We?"

"I'm going with you. If the roads are wet, you may want another driver."

When she didn't answer, he added, "Besides, what am I supposed to do in the meantime? You've already told me you don't want me alone in the shop."

To Hunter, her silence meant she'd backed herself into a corner. Let her think it over for a while. She'd see the good sense in taking him along. Instead, she muttered something and walked into the house.

As he turned, something white caught his eye. On the floor were folded papers.

He scooped them up. A two-page invoice from the insurance company indicated the amount Rae had received.

An insulting amount. And the records of various withdrawals, too, matching the days Benton had deposited money in his account.

Hunter shut his eyes, his stomach tightening into a hard knot. That explained where the money in his account had come from. And Rae's dark, worried look after her meeting.

Benton's trips into Moncton now made

sense. Green Valley lay west of the city, the penitentiary to the southeast. The old man hadn't just been coming to see Hunter, or his doctor. He'd been driving to town to deposit money into Hunter's account.

Had he gotten the money from his insurance policy?

The knot rose into Hunter's throat, and he swallowed hard to keep from choking. His bankbook's plastic case bit into his chest from the pocket of his jacket. Wait. Benton had only deposited half of the money he'd withdrawn. Where was the rest?

The kitchen door banged. When Hunter looked up, he saw Rae striding back toward the workshop, stirring up the oak and poplar leaves. Sadness was stamped upon her face. She had a contract to complete, money to earn, debts to pay. But it had been Hunter who'd encouraged Rae to take the work and any risks associated with it.

Risks such as a stranger luring her deep into the New Brunswick backwoods with rare lumber he seemed to know she desperately needed. A stranger who knew Benton. Could he be —

Rae entered the shop. Hunter met her steely gaze. "Let's get that wood," he stated.

"I already told you —"

"The wind's starting up and we can

expect heavy rain. You want to get it today, so I'm going with you. It would be foolish to go alone." He straightened, keeping his gaze even. *Lord, give her wisdom. Please don't force me to remind her that I own one half here.*

She nodded slowly. "All right."

He liked that she was finally being sensible. "We'd better go now. It may take us some time to find this place."

The drive into the sparsely populated countryside west of the national park was as silent as the morning's trip into town.

Just as well. A mat of dark clouds had blanketed the southwestern sky. By the time they hit the back roads, steady rain was falling. Hunter caught a glimpse of Rae's tight jaw, her white knuckles gripping the steering wheel. "You want me to drive?" he offered.

Despite the serious rainfall, poor visibility and unknown roads, Rae laughed.

"Sorry." She couldn't help herself. The absurd question seemed to come from nowhere. Biting her lips to stop her giggles, she added, "You haven't driven in years, and before that, you had your license for how long?"

A lopsided smile tipped up his mouth.

"Let's see, I was taken into custody when I was just over eighteen — and tried as an adult, I might add. I was held for almost a year until my sentencing, then immediately incarcerated. Before that, it took me three tries to get my license, which I finally got when I was seventeen and a half, so I had it for almost a year. So, are you going to let me drive?"

Again, she laughed out loud. "Six months' experience? You figure it out."

"Almost a year. Those extra five months can make a difference, you know."

She caught his grin as she flicked the windshield wipers on high. A short blast of hard rain swept past, tempering their humor. "Your reintroduction to driving shouldn't be during the remains of a hurricane." She paused, then added, "Maybe tomorrow, when it's dry out, you can drive into town."

"Gee, that's swell, Mom, thanks!" His grin made her catch her breath. Hunter had grown into a compelling, handsome man. In prison, of all places. She was nuts to notice, crazy to allow a winning smile to grip her heart. But she couldn't stop it.

She slowed for a nasty bend, spotted a sign pointing to a gravel side road and thanked God they were nearly there.

A mile farther, a wooden sign rocked in the wind. Being nestled deep in the woods wasn't protection against the storm. Rae drove up to a small, ancient trailer. A single oil lamp lit the left window.

The battered scraps of canopy on the old trailer flailed in the harsh wind, tossing off the rain like a shaggy dog shakes off bathwater. Through the heavy downpour, her headlights illuminated a yard littered with derelict equipment, some of it already being swallowed by the encroaching forest.

The door of the trailer banged open and a man in a dark green rainsuit hurried out. When he reached her, she rolled down the window.

Cutter Stevenson was a short, stocky man with a wild crop of white hair and thick glasses in front of his watery eyes. The wind tugged at his battered slicker, one bold gust snatching the smell of stale cigarettes and strong liquor and flinging it into the truck.

Rae found herself thankful that she'd brought Hunter.

"Rae Benton, eh? I didn't expect to see you in this rain." The old man coughed into her cab.

She leaned away. "I hadn't expected the rain to start so soon. Cutter Stevenson, I presume?"

"It's really Wallace, but working in the woods gets you a name like Cutter." He peered at Hunter, then looked back at Rae.

"This is Hunter Gordon."

The old man flicked a calculating glance at Hunter's frame before speaking again. "Well, come on into the shed. That's where the wood is."

With a short nod, he tugged on his hood and hurried to a small structure at the right of the trailer.

She rolled up the window. "I guess he approves of you."

Hunter pulled up the hood of his own jacket. "He was sizing me up. Deciding whether or not he should test the waters." He threw open his door and dashed out.

She bit her lip. Cutter Stevenson was curious, nothing more. Wasn't he? Her father's warning returned, and abruptly, a prayer popped into her head. *Keep us safe, please, Lord.*

She killed the engine as another barrage of rain peppered the windshield. It was going to be miserable loading the wood.

Her head bent, she slipped out and plowed across the yard toward the shed. Hunter held the door open for her as she stepped inside.

The shed was dry, and filled with the

scents of cedar and pine. Cutter was filling the small, potbellied stove with wood scraps and newspaper, and within a minute, heat filled the space. He'd lit a hurricane lamp and set it on a small plastic patio table. It threw long shadows around the room. Various lengths of raw wood lay stacked along the walls.

Hunter stood near the door with his arms folded. If Cutter noticed his suspicious posture, he didn't react. "Let me get that wood," he said, busying himself by tugging out short lengths of pine. "I was sorry to hear about your dad. Cancer's a wicked disease, for sure."

Hunter straightened, and Rae frowned. "When was the last time you saw my father, Mr. Stevenson?"

"It was about a month ago, at a gas station. He'd been down to Dorchester," he answered.

Rae couldn't stop her swift glance at Hunter. He appeared unmoved by Cutter's comment.

The old man pulled out another few pieces of wood. "Yup. Seen him at the pen several times over the last few years when I was delivering wood there." He paused. "Or was it the hospital? My arthritis is as bad as my memory." He held up his gnarled left hand.

All the while, his right hand remained behind the pile of wood. Rae still hadn't seen any bird's-eye maple. "Yup, knew your dad well enough to do some of his dirty work. Stuff I shouldn't have done."

A cold little shiver trickled through her. Beside her, Hunter tensed.

"Your dad could talk a dog off a meat wagon, promising me good money for my work. But not paying."

He pulled out a shotgun and aimed it at Rae's midsection. "So I'm asking for the money right now."

SEVEN

Immediately, Hunter shoved Rae behind him. In the dimness, with the hurricane lantern flickering, the old man was no match for him, he knew. The guy was half-drunk. But the shotgun gave him the advantage.

"Why don't you put that gun down and we'll do this the sensible way?"

Cutter hefted the weapon. "No way. I know about you. Benton talked of you, sayin' he was goin' to see you. That you'd worked for him before you burned his place down."

Hunter bristled. Behind him, Rae shifted, but he locked her in place with his left hand. She grabbed it and squeezed.

"Okay, then," he said. "What exactly do you want?"

"The money. All of what I said on the phone. I gave her a price for the wood. Said it was cash only."

Keep him talking, Hunter told himself, *until you can figure out how to get Rae safely out of here.* Was this the threat Benton had hinted at? But why not just tell them not to deal with Cutter Stevenson?

"How much did Benton owe you?"

"Seven thousand dollars, but I'm gonna need an even ten. That's what I told her."

Hunter gaped toward the wood beside Cutter. "Just for wood? Are you kidding?"

Behind him, Rae whispered, "Bird's-eye maple now costs about sixty-five dollars a linear foot. Dad was going to charge the contractor one hundred a foot for the spindles. I wasn't surprised when Cutter quoted that amount to me."

" 'Cept I know she has more money. Benton had more, selling that wood he stole."

"My father didn't steal anything!"

Hunter gripped her hand to keep her behind him. "Let's not throw accusations around, okay? I was with Rae when she went to the bank. She has what you asked for, so you can put down the gun."

The moment stretched, but the man didn't move. Hunter kept talking. "She's just buried her father. Give her a break."

"I want what's coming to me."

You'll get it, Hunter thought.

"I left the money in the truck," Rae whispered.

Cutter lifted the weapon. Hunter hadn't stared down the barrel of a gun since his first foster parents had died. At ten years of age, he'd been too small to do anything. His foster mother had shoved him behind the couch that day, before her husband raced toward the enraged biological father of one of the other foster kids. As soon as the man had killed the adults, he'd fled, leaving Hunter clinging to the back of the worn sofa.

"Get the money," Cutter ordered, interrupting the painful memory. "Gordon stays here. And if you try anything stupid, I'll kill him. Got that?"

Wide-eyed, Rae nodded. She backed away from Hunter; who did his best to shield her as she reached for the door. As soon as she opened it, a blast of wind and rain blew in. The oil lamp wobbled as the strong gust rocked the plastic table.

Cutter lunged for the lamp, obviously afraid it would topple over.

Hunter reacted, wrenching the gun from the man's hand. Once it was free, he swung it through the damp air until it connected with the woodsman's flabby cheek. Cutter let out a gurgling moan and fell against the table. The lamp wobbled again, but Hunter caught it before it could tip, lifting the glass and blowing out the flame. The shed sank into darkness.

Hunter ran outside, colliding with Rae on the broken fieldstone step. "Get into the truck! Start the engine. Now!"

She complied, and as he raced around to the passenger side, he flung the shotgun toward the woods, then jumped into the cab.

Rae gunned the engine and they were gone.

They said nothing as she sped along the gravel road. Reaching the provincial highway, she hesitated.

"Turn left," Hunter said, noting her disorientation.

Nodding shakily, she obeyed.

They traveled in silence for a while, until she let out a small gasp.

"What's wrong?" he asked.

She swiped at her eyes. "I can't drive! I'm starting to shake."

"Pull over. Take it easy. That's it. . . ." Hunter watched as she slowed the truck, easing it to a stop along the rain-soaked shoulder. Rae collapsed onto the steering wheel.

He pulled her into an awkward embrace. "It's all right."

She jerked back. "All right? That man was going to kill us! Look at me, I'm shaking all over! No one has ever pointed a gun at me before. Never!"

She *was* shaking. Her voice, her hands, her bottom lip. She shut her eyes. For a long minute they sat there with the rain beating down on them, until she leaned forward to shut off the engine and lights.

"How did you get the gun away from him?" she asked at last.

"When you opened the door, the wind shoved that plastic table back. Cutter reached over to stop it, and I snatched the gun."

"He could have shot you!"

"I'm stronger and faster." Hunter left out the part where he'd smacked the old man with the butt.

"But the lantern got knocked over."

"I caught it before it tipped, then blew it out, so it wouldn't set fire to the shed." Noticing she was still shaking, he leaned forward. "Rae, I don't like sitting here so close to that guy's house. I'll get out, you scoot over and I'll drive home."

She gave a small nod and said, "I guess your reintroduction to driving *is* going to be in a rainstorm."

He grinned. "I promise not to put it in

the ditch, Mom."

She smiled back, but her lips quivered. Hunter threw open the door and raced around the front of the truck, slowing for a brief moment to check the road. Inside, Rae scrambled across the bench seat to the passenger side.

It wasn't until they were east of the national park and minutes from home that she spoke again. "You were right."

"About what?" he asked.

"About me being in danger. I didn't believe you. I'm sorry."

"It's okay. It's not like it happens all the time. I'm here to keep you safe." He winked at her, trying to lighten the moment.

The mood lifted somewhat, until they reached her place. No sooner had they walked into the workshop than she turned and frowned at him. "What happened back there, Hunter? What was Cutter talking about? If Dad owed him money, why wouldn't he just submit a claim to Mr. Le-Blanc? Why did he say Dad was selling wood illegally?"

Hunter busied himself making a fire in the woodstove. "Because he has no claim and was trying to take advantage of you." Nice mild answer. Safe answer.

She handed him a small tin of matches

from the shelf behind the desk. "But Cutter said Dad was visiting you. Is that true?"

Don't ask, Hunter warned silently as he stacked kindling. The idea of lying to her tightened his throat. "Cutter also admitted that his memory was as bad as his arthritis."

"Answer my question."

"Cutter's an old drunk, Rae."

"Drunkenness loosens the tongue."

"He's a thief who was trying to rob us. He'd say anything to get what he wanted." Hunter rubbed his forehead, feeling his headache from the morning returning. "Look, he probably remembered my name from before, maybe even remembered that I went to prison. He was likely trying to divide us."

The fire started, and he shut the stove door. Rae had shed her raincoat and was rubbing her arms. That hollow look in her eyes reflected the shock that still lingered.

"We should go back to the police," she told him quietly. "I didn't even try to get them to take the threat seriously, but I can't ignore it now. But they're going to ask why Cutter would try to rob us. He was going on about Dad getting him to do his dirty work. We'll have to tell them that."

Hunter stood slowly. "Rae, he was drunk and has a bad memory. I wouldn't put too much stock in what he said, okay? Tell the police that, too."

She opened her mouth to answer, but he laid a hand on her shoulder. Her bones felt small and fragile under his fingers. "Trust me on this one, Rae."

Her gaze drifted up to his. The woodstove crackled and popped over the steady thrumming of the rain outside. He watched Rae swallow.

"Okay."

Victory surged through him. She might not trust him on everything, but after this, she'd taken a small, hopeful step forward.

The rain had eased by the time they drove to the village. Rae had handed him the truck keys wordlessly and climbed in the passenger side.

Hunter appreciated the gesture. A small thank-you for the drive home. "I need to stop by the grocery store after the police station," he said.

When she nodded, he drove straight to the station. Hunter had half hoped that Mike Halloway, who'd once suggested a youth crime prevention program to him in prison, would be on duty, but he wasn't. Instead, his partner interviewed them, then excused himself.

He returned a few minutes later. "It's not unusual for our patrols to check on some of the hermits around, especially during a storm. They did stop by Cutter's trailer tonight."

Hunter straightened. "He had at least one shotgun."

"All the officer found was the guy passed out. He didn't see any weapons, but you can be sure when he returns he won't go alone. And he'll find that firearm."

Hunter knew the police force was stretched so thin that many officers patrolled alone. Shrugging, he led the way out to the truck and opened the passenger door for Rae, then drove to the grocery store.

Rae took the keys from him. "I promised Annie I'd return her skirt suit. I'll come back for you in half an hour."

"Thanks." Hunter strode into the brightly lit store. Grabbing a basket, he began to check off a mental list of things he wanted. Fresh fruit, another thick steak —

"Hey."

He turned and found himself eye to eye with Mike Halloway. Hunter's first reaction was to the constable's uniform, but when he saw the offered hand, he stuck out his own.

"How's Ms. Benton?"

"We ran into a bit of trouble tonight. Your partner knows."

Halloway lifted an eyebrow. "I'll stop by the station."

A silence settled between them, interrupted only by a sharp squeal from some distant shopping cart. "How's your chest?" Mike asked at last.

Years ago, the inmate's knife had been sharpened with the officer in mind. Hunter had stopped a fatal stabbing with his own chest.

"I'll need surgery to loosen the scar tissue, but it's okay for now."

Halloway stepped to the left to allow a harried young mother with a crying child to plow past. His voice dropped. "I heard you own half of Benton Woodworking."

Before Hunter could reply, the officer's attention was caught by something at the back of the store. Hunter turned, noticing a teenager standing by the bulk candy bins.

"Remember the job I offered you?" Halloway stated, shifting topics. "I'm part of a team starting that program to educate teenagers about life behind bars. A deterrent, hopefully."

"And you want me as a speaker?"

Halloway laughed as he reached for a bag of carrots. Tossing them into his cart, he answered, "I want you to run the thing."

"Run it?"

"I can get the funding. There's one catch, though."

A wave of cold washed over him. "What is it?"

"This is a national program. You'll need to move out west. It's a bigger problem there than down east. But the pay's good, and the job even has some benefits."

Hunter stared at the boy, who was slyly filling his pockets with candy. Somewhere in the store a child screamed, and the PA system blurted out a request for parcel pickup. The wiry teen's mouth was full of pilfered sweets, a reflection of Hunter himself fifteen years ago.

He could never allow another kid to face what he'd gone through in prison.

"Mickey!" Halloway called over to the teen. With a flash of alarm, the boy chucked a stolen candy back into a bin. "Come here!"

The youth shuffled over. "Yeah?" As an afterthought, he added, "Sir?"

"I want you to meet someone. Hunter, this is Mickey Thompson. Mickey, this guy is Hunter Gordon. He's moved back from Dorchester."

The name of the pen caught the boy's

interest. Halloway continued, "Your mom here?"

Mickey nodded.

"Then go help her, and stay out of the candy. My groceries cost enough as it is."

Flicking a look at Hunter, the boy ambled around the corner to the next aisle.

Hunter spoke first. "Did you plan to have that kid here?"

The constable grinned widely. "No, but it was a great coincidence, don't you think?"

He didn't. As a Christian, Hunter didn't believe in coincidences. Yes, the job offer was enticing, all right. Enticing enough to leave Rae? After tonight?

A new life, a new start. The chance to use the gifts and experience God had given him. *Is this what you want of me, Lord? To leave Rae?*

He looked at Halloway. "Let me think about it."

"Good. I'll send over the details when I get a chance. I think you'll like this offer." The officer pushed his cart around the corner, leaving Hunter to battle his indecision.

He looked up, not surprised to see that Mickey had gravitated back to the candy. With a shake of his head, Hunter walked over. "Not only will that stuff rot your teeth, it'll also start you on a road you don't want to travel."

Bold now that Halloway had left, the boy glowered. "I ain't doing anything you ain't done. You just got out of prison. My folks talked about you."

Sympathy surged through Hunter, but he folded his arms. "Good for them. Now get away from that stuff."

"It's just a few. They charge too much for them, anyway."

"Next thing you'll be doing is scoring some dope somewhere."

The teen laughed. "You want dope? I can get you some right now."

He was ready to tell him not to bother, when the boy's attention flicked behind Hunter. He turned. Rae stood there, her scowl darker than the rain outside.

He heard Mickey snicker. "So much for you scoring some dope today, mister."

EIGHT

Ice coated Rae's stomach. Even before she'd entered the store, she'd spied Hunter finishing a conversation with Constable Halloway.

Hunter immediately crossed the produce section toward the town's most disreputable youth. Rae reached them in time to hear Mickey telling him he wouldn't be scoring any dope that day.

As soon as the boy spotted her, Hunter had turned.

She wanted to rush over and tell him how stupid he was being. But lashing out at him, as she had the other day, would achieve nothing.

Was that why it hurt her so much?

It didn't, she told herself sternly. The emotion was simply a knee-jerk reaction to seeing a man ruin his life again.

And while she was tossing around accusations, her father had been foolish for hiding his illness, and leaving her out of the loop on so many things. . . .

Then dying on her.

Her posture so stiff she ached, she managed to say coolly, "I'll meet you in the truck," just as Mickey Thompson snickered.

Hunter had the grace to look guilty, she noted as she spun on her heel.

Back behind the wheel, watching Hunter pay for some groceries, Rae sent up a prayer, hoping to ease her tension. *Lord, what's going on?*

No answer came. Hunter was now striding toward the truck, his jacket open and a fresh onslaught of rain dampening his shirt. He chucked his two grocery bags onto the seat between them and climbed in.

"It's not what you're thinking, Rae."

"What am I thinking?"

"That I'm buying dope right after my release from prison."

She said nothing.

"Am I right?"

"Am *I* right?" She started the engine and drove onto the street. After several minutes, she found herself asking, "So if you weren't looking to buy dope, why were you talking to him?"

"I told him candy can rot his teeth."

"Dental hygiene's the last thing on Mickey

Thompson's mind. Why don't you just give him some money, so he can buy toothpaste?"

"The kid doesn't need money. He needs mentoring."

She kept on driving. This wasn't the first time that word had floated around Green Valley. The school was still trying to get a mentoring program running.

Because of the rain, she nearly missed her own driveway, and swerved in at the last minute. The weight of recent events, and especially the presence of the man beside her, suddenly pressed down on her shoulders, and she was glad she was home.

"I was just talking to the kid, Rae."

Hunter's soft words barely reached through her heavy thoughts. She blew out a long sigh. "Don't do anything foolish, Hunter. You've already wasted ten years."

He shook his head. "It wasn't a waste. I accepted Christ into my heart. I learned that God put me in prison to finally reach me."

"Finally?"

"Yes. I didn't have a mother who was a Christian, who would take me to church. None of my foster parents were saved, either."

With all that had gone on these last few

days, Rae hadn't given her own mother much thought, as she should have. But she was glad her father had finally been saved and was now with God. "Do you have any brothers or sisters?"

A shadow darkened his expression. "One older brother. I don't know where he is, but I trust God will bring us together again." After a pause, he continued, "Rae, this isn't about my family. This is about you trusting me. I know you don't want to, but I'm asking you to. I wasn't doing anything illegal. I met Constable Halloway a few years back. A couple of other inmates decided to teach him a lesson for arresting them. I saw it coming and shoved Halloway out of the way. The shank got me."

"Shank?"

"Prison lingo for a homemade knife. You've noticed the scars at my neck. That was part of the stabbing."

"And your face? Was that part of it, too?"

"In a way. In retaliation for saving Halloway, they pinned me down, cut me and poured salt and vinegar into the wound."

Rae cringed. "Didn't you fight back?"

He gave her a patient smile. "I did. In fact, I was denied parole because of that one instance."

She bit her lip. "Were you hurt badly?"

Hunter shook his head. "It stung like the devil, though. Anyway, when Halloway saw me today, we talked."

She felt her cheeks warm. *Hunter saved your life, too, Rae.* She threw open the truck door and dashed toward the workshop. As soon as she stepped over the threshold, heat blasted her, stalling her thoughts.

It shouldn't be this hot in the workshop. It shouldn't be warm at all. Yes, the last few days had been cold and damp, and they'd had a fire on tonight, but the shop should have chilled down by now.

The stove! Rae raced over, stopping just short of it. Even without touching the door, she knew it was dangerously hot.

"What's wrong?"

She turned to Hunter. "The stove. It's super hot. Did you stoke the fire before we left?"

"No." He sniffed the air. "It's so hot it could explode. Close off the damper and let it cool slowly."

She skirted the stove to reach for the damper in the pipe. The handle was hot to the touch. She was leaning down to adjust the one at the base of the firebox, when she stopped.

There were shavings under the stove. Still feeling the heat from the fire, she brushed them away and picked up a large one. It was fresh, belonging to the pile they'd swept up the other day. Hunter had bagged them for a neighbor who raised chickens.

Rae stood and glanced around until she spied the garbage bag Hunter had used to load up the shavings. Now empty, the bag lay over a garbage can.

She had seen Hunter take it outside. He'd even damp-mopped the floor afterward, to clean up the sawdust. "I think someone has loaded this stove with shavings."

Hunter went instantly alert. "Come on! Let's get out of here!"

She didn't need convincing. Too many shavings were dangerous. Gases could build up and explode in the basic stove, and through the tiny window she could see the smoldering shavings waiting for a draft of air to ignite them further.

Hunter snatched her arm as they hurried outside. There was nothing they could do but starve the stove of air and let the fire cool and die. Rae turned to face the workshop.

Please, Lord, don't let it burn down.

Standing out in the pouring rain, she looked up at Hunter. "Do you think Cutter could have done this?"

"There was no vehicle there, and you

113

heard the police officer say they saw him. He was sleeping off a binge. Even if he had a car or truck, he couldn't have come here."

"Then who?"

Hunter said nothing. Facing him, Rae met his gaze squarely. "What, Hunter? What are you thinking?"

"That he has friends."

Grabbing the grocery bags, Rae started toward her house. "Let's get out of the rain. We'll put your groceries in my fridge, okay?"

Once inside, she set Hunter's foodstuffs on a refrigerator shelf. "What illegal thing was my father doing?"

He crushed the plastic sacks. "I don't know, Rae. And that's the truth. I've been in prison."

She clutched his arm. "But Dad visited you. Did he go there regularly?"

Hunter didn't tug his arm away. "Please don't ask, Rae. I'm not proud of my past, but I've learned from it. So just trust me."

She remembered the funeral, how she'd wanted to toss him out of the chapel. She also remembered their conversation a few minutes ago. He was like her in many ways, and yet had so much faith that God was directing his path. Part of her admired him and wanted to trust him.

Another thought struck her. Someone had

tampered with the stove, wanting it to explode. Hunter hadn't done it this time.

Was it possible he hadn't done it ten years ago?

Regardless of her silent questions, she nodded. She wouldn't ask about Dad's visits to the pen. At least not yet.

Hours later, when the stove was cool enough to open, Hunter shoveled the ashes into a bucket. After snatching up some receipts he'd knocked off the desk, he walked outside to dump the ashes into a large barrel at the edge of the woods. He returned and mopped up any more that he'd spilled. When he went back outside to hang up the mop, he found Rae standing there.

She wet her lips. Something was coming. Anticipation clutched at him.

"Hunter, I want to say something. . . ." She trailed off and he found himself holding his breath.

Tell her what you tried to say to that boy, Mickey. Tell her about Constable Halloway and his new program.

Tell her the truth, Gordon.

The last suggestion caught in his throat. Her mouth a tight line, she walked up to him, and only then did he realize she was preparing to eat crow.

"Um, how's your headache?" she began.

"Still there, but the fresh air helps. Is there something you want to say?"

"I assumed you were looking to buy dope or break the law. I just saw you with Mickey and jumped to conclusions. I'm sorry. It's been an awful week. I have no money to pay my bills. Dad must have spent his insurance money on cancer treatments, though I never saw anything and . . ." She faltered. "And I can't believe he wouldn't tell me he was so sick. He was always trying to protect me."

There they were, facing each other, Rae with her hands clutched in front of her, and him gripping the shovel's handle as if his life depended on it.

Tell her about the money. Tell her everything.

No. All she had now were good memories of her father.

She took another step toward him. *How can you keep the truth from her?* Benton had willed him more than he'd willed his own flesh and blood. Rae would ask why, leaving Hunter with the choice of either lying to her or hurting her more with the truth.

Sweat broke out on his forehead.

The scent of roses soothed some of the chaos in him. He couldn't tell her. But there she was, standing innocently in front of him.

116

He dropped the shovel but never heard it thud to the ground. One short step with open arms and he'd pulled her into a tight embrace.

A few minutes later, Rae tilted her head back. He lowered his own and met her lips with a searing kiss.

When she tightened her own arms, he stiffened. What was he doing? He should be ministering to her, not kissing her. Reluctantly, he eased away.

"Don't say you're sorry you kissed me, Hunter," she whispered through the quiet drizzle that had begun to fall again. "I know you want to, but I don't want to hear it."

"It was only meant to be a comforting hug."

"Oh, well, aren't you good for a girl's ego?"

Despite the serious moment, he chuckled. "Your charm, not to mention your bashfulness, changed my mind."

It was her turn to laugh, though hers was much more reserved. She murmured, "I did want to kiss you."

"Only as an affirmation."

"Of what?"

"It's not uncommon to look for ways to reaffirm that you're still alive. Some people do it by plunging themselves into work, or doing something fast and hard, some by running from God."

After considering his words, he added, "Most people will admit that when dealing with death or grief, they often attempt to reaffirm their own life. Do something they wouldn't normally do."

"I can hear a 'but' coming."

He shrugged. "No. Grief scares us. It forces us out of our comfort zones."

She pulled back her shoulders. "I know all the stages of grief. I've been down this road with my mother. All I wanted was a kiss, Hunter. Please don't deny me that small thing."

With that, she returned to the workshop.

NINE

The morning sun the next day warmed Hunter's face as he stood at the end of the driveway. He'd gone for a jog. Feeling the wind on his face, he'd pushed himself past that unseen wall and gone the extra mile. He'd missed running all the years he'd been in prison, the burn in his lungs. He didn't mind the blackout he'd experienced or the stupid stumble on a rock that had resulted from it. His palms and knees were scraped and bloodied, but he felt good.

With his hands splayed on his thighs, he pulled in a deep breath of the crisp, frosty dawn air.

A noise caught his attention and he snapped his head up. Andy Morrison had just parked his car along the road beside the house. Hunter straightened as the man alighted.

"I know a whole lot more than you think I do," Morrison said as he reached Hunter.

"About what?" he panted.

"About you and Rae's father. I know what you two did before you burned the shop down."

Hunter folded his arms. His hands stung, but he ignored them. "And that was what?"

"It's illegal to harvest trees from public land without a permit."

"Thanks for the tip."

"I can get you into a lot of trouble. They've found a way to match lumber to its stump. I know Benton and you were stealing bird's-eye maple. It's a lucrative business."

Yes, that was why Benton had suggested it. And young and foolish as he had been back then, Hunter had agreed. He'd been swayed by greed and influenced by the warped logic that the trees belonged to them because they were on public land. Benton had known someone who could recognize bird's-eye maple just from the bark. If not for that, the tree would have to be cut down before anyone else could recognize the valuable wood. It had all added up to an offer that Hunter accepted eagerly.

Someone Benton knew? Hunter blinked. Was that person Cutter Stevenson?

"And I know a whole lot more about what

you two were involved in after," Morrison growled.

After? "What do you want?"

"Let me be blunt. All I want is a chance with Rae. But as long as you're around, that isn't happening. Take off. I don't care where you go, as long as you don't stick around here."

"And if I don't?"

"Then I'll tell her what kind of person you really are." Morrison laughed. "Yeah, I know you haven't told her anything. And I'll tell the police a few things, too, just for added incentive."

"Such as?"

"You know. Benton didn't visit you in prison out of guilt. You two were planning things. I don't buy that you got saved." The man leaned forward, almost touching Hunter's nose. "Don't stand in my way, Gordon. Or you'll regret it." For added effect, he swung his arm to punch him.

All the self-control he'd ever learned was needed now, but it wasn't enough. Hunter grabbed Morrison's shirt collar and hauled him back to his car, yanking open the door and shoving him inside.

Morrison's head fell back as Hunter let him go. It bounced off the seat and then forward into the steering wheel. When he lifted it again, his nose was bleeding.

Hunter frowned. He was handling this badly, but he wasn't going to be intimidated by this little weasel. He leaned forward, fully aware that he was risking the tenuous trust he was building with Rae.

Too bad. Her life was more important, and it looked right now as if Morrison might be the person Benton had wanted him to watch out for.

"Get lost, Morrison. If I see you around here again, I'll call the cops myself. I have nothing to hide from them."

"Yeah, right. You're both going to regret this, Gordon. You and Rae."

The man spat out something rude, and spun his wheels as he sped off.

"Hunter! What's going on?"

Hunter walked up the driveway toward Rae, who frowned at him in the morning light. "Nothing. Morrison stopped by to tell me to take off."

She looked perplexed. Then, horrified, she noticed his hands. "Did he hurt you?"

"This," he said, holding up his palms, "is what happens when you run too hard and trip on a rock. I went jogging this morning. With Morrison, I merely helped him get back into his car. He did take a swing at me."

"Because you refused to leave?"

"Sort of. I think he may be involved somehow with Cutter Stevenson. He inferred he could get me into a lot of trouble, saying something about tree theft, and that makes me think of Stevenson. If I left Green Valley, Morrison said, he wouldn't tell you or the police."

Rae came closer, her brows knitted. "You've been in prison for ten years. How could you be involved with anything like that?"

Hunter didn't want to lie, but to tell the truth meant he'd have to say he believed her father had been breaking the law for years. He frowned. "All I know is he said he knew what was going on, and would tell you and the police if I didn't leave."

"Let him. Then maybe we'd find out who's trying to hurt me. In fact, we should call his bluff. Go to his office and confront him."

At the mention of that, Hunter led her back up the driveway. "No. There's more going on here than we know, and I won't risk your life."

He stopped, remembering something, then stepped into the shop. She followed. It

123

was cold and quiet in there, and he walked straight to the desk. On top, where he'd set it, was a receipt. "Do you know anything about this?"

Rae took the slip and read it. "It's a restaurant in Moncton, isn't it? I've never been there."

"It's a small café not far from where Morrison works. It's where your dad first met me."

"Really?"

"Yes. I found this receipt when I was cleaning out the stove. Maybe it fell out of someone's pocket when he was looking for matches."

"Let's go there. We'll ask who orders . . ." she glanced at the paper ". . . the breakfast sandwich with hot chocolate. If it's Morrison, then we'll take this to the police."

The restaurant was pretty much as Hunter had described it. Rae stepped around a table where some businessmen sat drinking coffee. The smells of bacon and toast filled her nostrils, reminding her that she'd missed breakfast.

As they headed for the counter, they scanned the crowd, but didn't see Morrison. Perhaps he'd forgone breakfast, if it was he who had come here at all.

"What'll it be? Coffee?"

Hunter smiled at the waitress as they sat at the counter. "For both of us, please. I was hoping to meet my friend here today, but don't see him. He usually orders your breakfast sandwich with hot chocolate."

"Oh, him. You missed him. Today he took his order to go. Sorry." She poured the coffee.

"That's too bad," Hunter continued, taking a sip from his mug. "I heard he'd been in a fight and got a nosebleed."

The waitress dropped small creamers and packets of sugar onto the counter. "That's probably why he didn't stay. He didn't want to bleed all over my station."

"So it's true?"

The woman lifted her bony shoulders. "Well, his nose was red and it sure looked like he'd been roughed up. He went to the washroom to clean up while I got his order together. I hope he hasn't made a mess in there." With that, she left.

"It was Andy!" Rae hissed. "He was in the shop without us knowing it. He must have set the fire!"

Hunter shrugged, looking nonchalant. "Drink up. We're going to his workplace."

They quickly downed their coffees, then Hunter left a generous amount on the counter for the waitress. Outside, they hurried around the corner to the government office where Andy worked.

Rae found her heart pounding. *Keep us safe, please, Lord. Whatever it is that we must do, let us do it for You.*

The office was almost vacant, with the one person ahead of them finished seconds after they entered. Hunter walked to the counter, introduced himself and Rae, and asked to see Andy.

"He wasn't feeling well, so he left," the man behind the counter answered. "Rae Benton, you say?"

"Yes," she answered. "Is there something wrong?"

"Nothing." After glancing down at Hunter's scraped hands, the man stepped back a bit. "The name rings a bell, that's all."

"I know Andy. He lives in Green Valley, like I do. Maybe he's mentioned me?"

The man's expression stayed cool. "That's probably it. Can I give Andy a message for you?"

Hunter shook his head. "No, thanks, we'll stop by another time."

Outside, he looked pensive. "What's wrong?" Rae asked.

"I don't like the way that guy knew your name."

She didn't answer. The short conversation hadn't felt right to her, either. They returned to the truck, both deep in thought.

"Should we report this?" she finally asked.

"Yes."

"But we're behind in that contract. We can't afford to lose any more time at the police station." She leaned forward. "Hunter, what do we have for evidence? You already cleaned out the stove and mopped the floor. This receipt means nothing, and Andy could easily say it fell out of his car when he came by to visit me. He could add that you instigated the disagreement."

She hated that they had such little proof, and regret swamped her as she thought of her earlier nonchalance. "Let's wait and see what Andy does next. We'll be on guard, ready for it."

"He probably isn't alone in this, Rae."

She smiled. "Nor are we."

They spent the remainder of the day working on the contract, forcing the strange morning into the back of their minds. The next day passed without incident, and by the end of it, Rae was thankful she had her work to concentrate on.

She had to find a source of bird's-eye

maple, now that Cutter wasn't going to provide it. Rae chewed her lip, not looking forward to telling her customer that there was going to be a delay. But she'd find a source, she decided firmly.

Everywhere around her were reminders of the danger her father had warned Hunter of. At least with work, she could do something to honor his memory.

Dusk was falling the next day when the growl of an engine penetrated the quiet shop. Both Rae and Hunter went to the door.

A police cruiser had come to a stop behind Rae's truck. Mike Halloway and his partner got out, their expressions dark.

Rae whispered, "What do you suppose they want?"

We'll find out soon enough, Hunter thought. He pushed open the door and warily stared at the men. Suddenly, the self-protective instinct he'd honed for years was on full alert. That familiar gut-clenching tightness almost hurt, and he turned to Rae with a rigid jaw.

"Stay inside," he muttered. He had no idea why; he just knew that he didn't want her to come out.

"Hunter," Halloway said quietly. Hunter

noticed the other officer's hand hovering over his sidearm. Halloway slowly reached behind him for something.

Handcuffs. Hunter had worn them enough to know where they were kept.

"We need you to come down to the station," Halloway told him calmly.

His instinct had been bang on the money. Hunter kept his hands where they could be seen, and his voice even. "Sure. What for?"

Halloway's expression turned grim. "We found Andy Morrison's car this morning, behind an abandoned building in Green Valley. Do you know anything about that?"

"No. You should ask Morrison."

"He hasn't been seen for a few days. You did go to his workplace and to his favorite restaurant, asking about him."

Hunter chose his words carefully. "He came around the other morning to hassle us. I wanted to tell him to back off. But he wasn't at either place."

"You weren't far behind, though, were you? The waitress at the restaurant reported that you'd missed Morrison by only a few minutes. And we found your blood on the door handle of his car."

"How do you know it's mine?"

The other officer answered, "We still have samples of your DNA from when you got stabbed. We also found a considerable amount of Andy Morrison's blood in the car."

"And you know it's his?"

"He'd shown up at work with a bloody nose and had thrown out the tissues he'd used before he left," the constable answered.

Halloway flicked out his handcuffs. "Turn around, hands behind your back, Hunter Gordon. You're coming with us."

Ten

Having slipped outside, Rae couldn't stop the gasp that escaped. As fast as she could, she raced over to the men.

"He couldn't have done it! Sure, he talked to Andy, but that was before work. Besides, Andy hasn't filed a complaint!"

"It's all right, Rae. I know the routine." Hunter turned his back and extended his wrists, refusing to look at her while he was being cuffed.

"Wait a minute! What evidence do you have?" Rae asked.

"We have sufficient evidence to bring him in for questioning," Halloway answered, looking at Hunter. "Did you kill Andy Morrison?"

"No." Hunter's voice was calm. "But I won't resist."

Panic struck Rae hard. She stepped forward to stare at him as he settled into the backseat of the cruiser. He didn't meet her eyes. "This is all wrong!" She spun toward the officers. "Morrison has been hitting on me for months, and Hunter just wanted to tell him to back off. That was it!" Despite her plea, or perhaps because of it, his expression changed. Halloway was thinking that she'd just provided them with motive.

The police officer ground his heel into the soft dirt of the driveway and strode around the cruiser. Before he climbed inside, he called over the top, "He'll phone you, Ms. Benton. He'll give you some details on a lawyer or bail."

Quickly, he averted his eyes and got in.

He'd call? They expected her to just stay here and carry on as if nothing was wrong? "Wait!" She rushed up to the car, grabbing the driver's window as Halloway rolled it down. "This is ridiculous! Hunter's been with me for two days, working!"

Halloway remained calm and respectful. "He'll call. We're going to ask some questions, and he can give a statement."

"Can I come along?"

"No!" It was Hunter who snapped out the answer. He leaned forward. "Stay here, Rae. Everything will be fine. I'll call. Just do some paperwork or something. And lock the doors!"

Grim-faced, Halloway backed up the cruiser.

By the time it reached the road, the truth had sunk in and she felt hot tears rolling down her cheeks.

A cool draft followed and she wiped her face with her hands. Why was she wasting tears? Hunter didn't want her to come with him.

Hating the helplessness, she shuffled back inside to stare at her desk. Hunter had told her to finish up some paperwork, but how could she? Her mind numb, she sank into her chair and picked up her pen.

An age later, the screech of brakes penetrated her foggy state. By the time she looked up, Annie, a pained expression on her face, was bustling over the threshold into her shop, with Kirk holding the door open.

As much as Rae loved her cousin, she knew she could overdramatize circumstances. Annie's shocked expression looked almost farcical, considering her pageboy hairstyle. With his own brown hair slicked back, Kirk remained stone-faced as usual.

Annie broke the silence. "We were at the gas station and Edith Waterbrook told us Hunter had been seen getting dragged into the police station! Is it true?"

Rae checked her watch. Seven in the evening.

Oh, Hunter, why haven't you called?

"You should have phoned us!" Annie was about to slip off her jacket when she shivered. She pulled it closer. "Good grief, you need some heat on in here if you're going to work. And the floor is damp, for honesty's sake!"

"I wasn't cold." Rae glanced toward the woodstove, unwilling to put on a fire. "Let's go in the house."

"Good idea. Kirk'll make some tea."

Kirk growled, "We don't need tea and cookies, Annie. Rae's fine. That bum is behind bars."

Irritation rose in Rae at his prickly words, but she told herself he was entitled to his opinion. Kirk had liked her father and had spent years sending business their way whenever the opportunity arose. In turn, her father had sent many customers to Kirk's small electrical shop.

It had all changed after the fire. Even Kirk's business seemed to have suffered over the last few years, and he'd become almost surly.

"*I'll* make tea. I could use a cup," Rae answered heavily.

After settling down with mugs of steaming tea, she explained what happened. Annie leaned across the table. "I love you dearly, Rae, but Hunter does seem the unsavory kind."

She took a swallow of her tea. "So's Andy Morrison. He's up to something. Why hasn't anyone found him?"

Annie's jaw dropped and she slapped her bosom with her left hand. "Found him? They're all saying he's dead."

"How would anyone know, if no one has found a body? Where did they find the car?"

Annie blinked. "Behind that old building near Edith Waterbrook's gas station. Half-hidden by trees."

Rae knew the area, just outside of the village. The forest was government — crown — land. And Andy Morrison was in charge of leasing crown land. "Seems strange. If a person wanted to hide a car, leaving it so close to town wouldn't cut it."

"Gordon would have heard of all the ways to stump the police." Kirk's voice, always forceful, bounced irritatingly around the kitchen. "Making it look like you're being framed would be one of them. Besides, it's easier to hide a body, than a car. And he'd have to hide the body, because it would have more evidence on it."

Annie stared at her husband with her

mouth open before snapping her attention back to Rae. "You have to come home with us."

She lifted her head. "Why?"

"Because you work with a murderer, and he could come back and kill you!"

"If he'd planned on murdering me, he'd have already done so. I'm fine. The one I should be concerned about is Morrison. Something is going on and I bet he's in the thick of it, if he's not hurt somewhere."

Kirk set his mug down. "No. Annie's right, Rae. Your business can do without you for a while."

"No, it can't. I have work to do."

"If this is a question of money —"

Rae scraped back her chair and jumped up. "It's not a question of money!"

She hated money. Dad had somehow spent his life insurance money, which she needed to keep her business going and pay her bills, including the funeral expenses. Now Kirk was offering cash, to lure her away from her home. Probably at Annie's suggestion . . .

Just like Christine Stanton tried to do.

Annie cut in. "This isn't about money. It's about your life. Get packed."

"I'm not going anywhere. Really. I'll lock the doors. Tomorrow, I'll even go to the

136

animal shelter and find a big dog for protection, if you like. But I'm not giving up and walking away! We didn't when this place burned down and I'm not going to now."

After a strained pause, she added, "Thank you, anyway."

"What about supper? When did you last eat?" Annie looked around the kitchen, settling her gaze in a plate that held two dried up date squares.

Rae rolled her eyes. If that was what it would take to be alone, she'd eat them. Leaning over, she grabbed both squares and shoved them into her mouth. They were so dry she had to wash them down with lukewarm tea. "Satisfied?"

Annie didn't appear convinced, but Kirk shrugged and drained his cup. "Whatever, Rae. But remember this. It was Hunter who burned down your workshop. He's already proved himself dangerous."

Rae lifted her mug and dumped the remaining tea down the drain in the sink. Kirk was hardly one to criticize anyone. Until he met Annie, he'd been an unsavory character himself, hanging out at taverns and nearly drinking himself into an early grave. Everyone knew Annie had straightened him out, even getting him to go to church periodically.

"Hunter didn't kill anyone," Rae said into the silence.

You accused him of murder, Rae.

The voice in her head sounded so clear, she nearly jumped.

Kirk was still talking. ". . . the police don't take people in for questioning. They must believe they have solid proof."

"So if they have this solid proof, they won't be letting Hunter go tonight. That means I'm safe."

Annie and Kirk said nothing. Rae gave an enormous yawn. "It's getting late and I'm wiped. I'll call you first thing in the morning, Annie, okay?"

Her cousin opened her mouth to protest, but Kirk stood. "Fair enough. Let's go, Annie. She's okay and that's what you came to find out. Rae, if you need us, call. I mean it."

"Thank you." Rae watched Annie follow her husband outside, hearing her muffled protests about him giving up too easily. Thankfully, Kirk knew neither of them would change her mind.

Dawn had long since seeped into her bedroom window, reminding Rae that she'd forgotten to close the curtains. She'd slept like the dead.

Bad choice of words. She stretched and threw off the covers, only to have pain stab into her temples.

Stress, she told herself. Half an hour later, having swallowed a painkiller, she turned to the phone in the kitchen. She'd promised to call Annie. But as she picked it up, a thought hit her. With her uncanny knack of judging a person's state of health by his or her voice, Annie would be over in a shot. She'd suspect that Rae was sick, and would insist on taking her home. Rae didn't want to leave, not with Hunter having promised to call.

Lord, keep him safe. Show the truth to the police, that Hunter didn't kill Andy.

The receiver waited silently in her hand.

Silently? She looked down at the phone, then lifted it to her ear.

Nothing. No dial tone. No busy signal.

She tapped the disconnect button. Nothing happened.

The line was dead.

The clock on the microwave said it was nearly noon. Hunter would have tried to get a hold of her by now. But with a dead phone, how could she know for certain?

Rae hurried back to the bedroom and tried the extension. Dead, too.

She'd try the one in the workshop. If it didn't work, and with no cell phone, she'd have to go into town, stop at the hardware store that hosted the phone company outlet, report the problem and then go straight to the police station. Constable Halloway could tell her if Hunter had been released, couldn't he?

A short scraping noise drew her attention. She started to spin around, but was stopped abruptly.

Something big and dark flew toward her, and a second later, she found herself pushed facedown into her pillow.

ELEVEN

Hunter climbed from the taxi with every bone aching. He was thankful that the police, on advice from the attorney general's office had released him. It had been an awful night, made worse by the fact he couldn't get a hold of Rae. Now, looking up the driveway, relief washed over him at the sight of her truck. She *was* home.

So why hadn't she answered her phone?

She hadn't wanted him to be near her the day she'd buried her father. Was the same true now?

Lord, let that not be true.

After paying the driver, Hunter remembered that she had wanted to come with him. He had told her to stay at home.

He rubbed the back of his neck, still sore from a sleepless night. Ignoring the goodbye beep from the cabbie, he walked up the drive.

Behind him, the workshop stood dark and

closed tight. The house didn't look any more welcoming. He headed for the door. It was unlocked? He peered at the latch, finding that both it and the locking plunger had been taped back. The door wouldn't lock.

The hairs on his neck tingled. He stepped into the kitchen. "Rae?"

Silence. Swiftly, he cataloged the sight before him. Three cups, all used, with a small plate with crumbs on it.

She'd had company. Who? Had she left with them? Hunter's scalp crawled as he called her name again. "Rae!"

Still no answer. Concern filled him, and he plowed through the kitchen and up the stairs. The front bedroom belonged to Rae, and he reached it in three long strides.

Her door stood open. He started at what he saw. Rae lay sprawled on the bed, facedown, one arm dangling over the edge. With a strangled gasp, he lunged toward her.

The door was flung against him, hitting him square in the face as he charged in. He felt the smack of its edge on his forehead and stumbled backward.

He yelled out, and a strong arm knocked him aside.

The intruder raced out.

Struggling to regain his footing, Hunter

glanced down the hall, but caught only a glimpse of a man lurching down the stairs. A breath later, he heard the back door swing open, then slam shut. A thump followed.

Forget it! Hunter whirled to face Rae, and raced over to lift her from the bed.

Her skin was blue.

In prison, he'd seen his share of death. By suicide, murder, even natural causes when an old lifer gave up the ghost.

Shock kicked Hunter into action now. He tilted her head back, lifted her chin and delivered a powerful breath into her lungs. Next, he checked her carotid artery, and, praise God, found a steady pulse.

Thank you, Lord.

Suddenly, she sucked in a deep, raspy breath, and her eyes flew open.

His heart pounding, he rolled her over onto her side, arranging her in the recovery position.

But the movement roused her, and she jerked away from him. For a moment, she blinked. With a frown and another swallow, she gasped, "Hunter? When did you get here? What time is it?"

"Nearly noon. What's going on? Why didn't you answer my calls?"

She took a moment to answer. "You didn't call. I waited all evening. Annie and Kirk were here," she added wearily, scrubbing her face.

Hunter helped her to sit on the edge of the bed, then sat down beside her. He caught a faint whiff of the sweet, fresh rose lotion she used, but forced himself to ignore it. "Tell me what happened. Who was here?"

Frowning, she tilted her head a moment. Then, a look of horror washing over her, she lunged off the bed.

She just made it to the bathroom before she threw up.

Hunter grabbed the cordless phone by her bed and dialed 911. Nothing happened. He clicked the receiver, but still heard nothing.

The line was dead. After smacking down the phone, he helped Rae back to bed. She lay there, eyes closed, but thankfully, a rosier pink had returned to her face.

"Did you see who was here?" she asked without opening her eyes.

"No." He wanted to kick himself for that, but there was no point now. "He was hiding behind the door, and took me by surprise. Did you let him in?"

"No. I got up, went into the kitchen and then remembered to call Annie. That was when I realized the phone was dead."

"Why Annie?"

"She and Kirk stopped by last night. They

144

were on their way to get groceries when they spotted the police taking you into the station. Annie insisted on driving straight here to find out what happened."

The three cups. "They had coffee?"

"Tea, actually. It took me some time to convince Annie that I was all right. She thought you were dangerous and trying to kill me."

The old sensitivities arose again and he bristled. What did he expect? He was a felon, fresh from prison after serving his full sentence because he'd fought too much and lost any chance at parole. He bit back the irritation, and said, "That was last night. What happened this morning?"

She flexed her neck. "I went back to the bedroom to see if the phone in here worked, but it didn't." She swallowed. "I turned and suddenly, there was . . . I don't know . . . something big flew at me. Then I was pushed down onto the bed. Facedown."

She shivered. Hunter tugged up the bedspread and wrapped it around her. She shrugged it off. "No. We've got to tell the police. Someone broke into my house, cut my phone lines and then tried to kill me! And he was too agile to be Cutter."

Hunter watched Rae try to stand, but her legs wobbled. With a strong arm, he steadied

145

her and led her down the hall. As they passed the coatrack by the back door, he grabbed her jacket, a tan-and-black one perfect for the fall. "We should take you to the doctor first."

"I'm fine. I was fighting quite a bit, so the guy couldn't keep me pinned down. He only had me there a few moments. I heard you call my name."

"He must have, too, and hid behind the door." Hunter clenched his jaw, and led her to the truck. After the trip to Cutter Stevenson's house, both sides of the truck body were caked with mud. But the right fender caught his eye. The mud was freshly smeared.

Whoever had tried to kill Rae had run into the side of the vehicle. As Hunter helped her into the cab, he scanned the ground. There were footprints, but yesterday, Halloway and his partner had come. And after, Annie and Kirk had come in and gone out. Hunter couldn't distinguish between the prints, with the exception of Rae's and her cousin's, whose feet were smaller.

When he climbed into the truck, Rae asked, "Why didn't you phone me last night?"

"They interrogated me for hours."

"But they didn't arrest you?"

"No. I told them what had happened, and they took pictures of my hands and knees. I think they found pieces of rock and dirt in the blood on the car, and knew that I was telling the truth. Besides, I don't have a motive to kill Morrison. All he wants to do is date you."

Rae shot him a furtive look, as if to gauge his reaction to that statement. *All he wants to do is date you.* Hunter's heart clenched. He didn't want Andy around. He didn't want anyone interested in Rae. Where had such strong feelings come from?

". . . and I was concerned when you didn't call."

Hunter snapped his attention back to Rae. "By the time I was allowed to call you, the line was dead."

"So whoever broke in this morning must have cut the phone line last night." She rubbed her temples as if she had a headache. "That doesn't make any sense. Why not try to smother me in the night? Why wait until morning?"

"I don't know. We'll find out, but first, let's go to the police." He threw her a small, wry smile. "I'm sure they'll be surprised to see me."

They were. But Halloway and the other officer listened intently to Rae. Hunter

147

breathed a small sigh of relief and said a grateful prayer.

Halloway left to see if the truck could reveal anything that might identify who had been in her house. The other officer took her statement, while another went over to her house. Hours later, with Rae looking ready to drop, Hunter asked if they could go home. It was nearly dark.

It still took another hour to finish up, sign papers and other things.

"You're free to go," Halloway finally reported. "Sorry it took so long. We fixed your back door lock because it had been taped, and we had the propane company come in and look at the furnace."

Rae appeared confused. "Why?"

"When we searched your house, we found that your furnace had been tampered with and the batteries removed from the propane detector. The propane tech we called said it looked like someone tried to reroute un-burned propane into your house."

Rae gasped. "I didn't smell propane. And I put fresh batteries in a month ago."

"Well, whatever they tried to do didn't work. There's a sensor in the furnace that detected the problem and shut the propane off at the tank. No propane ever leaked into the house, but there was evidence of tampering. Whoever tried to kill you must have realized this morning that he'd failed, and tried again with a pillow."

Halloway turned to Hunter. "The technician found the same tampering with the propane stovetop in your apartment."

"What kind of tampering?"

"Well, a grout sealant was dabbed under the jets. It looked like someone wanted to plug them and hopefully cause an explosion. But the sealant got burned off. However, the tech said that burning the sealant would have caused a dangerous gas to form."

Rae crept closer to Hunter. "What kind of dangerous gas?"

"Something that can be fatal if inhaled for too long. Or at least cause lethargy, headaches and disorientation." Halloway shook his head. "The tech said he knew what it was by its smell."

Hunter felt Rae's hand slip into his. "I used the stove the day of my release, and the next day had a headache," he murmured.

"So it must have been tampered with before your release." Halloway pulled out his notepad and wrote in it. "No one been in there besides you?"

"No. Only Rae, when she came in to wake me."

"You know we found a receipt from a restaurant that Andy Morrison goes to — there in the workshop," she stated. "For the very breakfast he orders every day. He had to be the one who tried to burn the shop down. And when it didn't work, he came back."

Obviously tired of the explanations, she added, "You should be looking for him. Someone tried to kill me, and tried to blow up my workshop again. Find Andy, and I bet you'll find your answers." That said, she folded her arms.

Halloway nodded, glanced at his partner and suggested quietly, "Why don't you two go home? If we need you, we'll stop by. And as for the phone, the company will send someone over tomorrow to fix it. I called them for you. Everything is fine."

Fine? Hunter didn't think so, but there was little that could be done tonight, and Rae needed to get home. He nodded and led her outside. This was becoming too serious. Too dangerous. What had Benton done to warrant this kind of danger?

Thankfully, there was no one around as they left the police station. Hunter held the passenger door for Rae, his stomach tight and fatigue weighing him down.

He thrust that aside, planning to make a full pot of coffee and turn that shop upside down until he found any and all clues to what Benton had got himself, and ultimately, Rae, into.

After she was safely asleep in bed.

Or he should send her to a hotel? One with excellent security, like the fancy one in downtown Moncton. He had enough money for just one night, since he'd transferred all Benton's money to Rae's account. She hadn't been to the bank since the transfer had cleared to realize that. If Hunter suggested a hotel room for her, she'd refuse, saying she couldn't afford it. And telling her that she could would mean he'd have to explain more than he had time for right now.

You don't want to destroy Benton's memory for Rae, do you?

He didn't. But he had to stop whoever was trying to kill her, and the only way to do that was to find out what Benton had graduated to in terms of illegal activities.

The wind nipped at Hunter, a chilly breeze from the bay that had already brought another shower light enough to grease the road. Hard to believe it had been so warm just a few days ago.

Hunter climbed in. Inside the truck, he

said, "I'm sorry for all that's happening, Rae. I'm sorry for everything. I wish things could have been different."

"But why me? I haven't done anything wrong, and all of a sudden, God is dumping on me."

"Rae, I know it's difficult, and it's going to take a while to get over it all, but you will. We'll figure this out."

Her chin quivered as she shut her eyes. "This is not your concern, Hunter."

It was. She wanted to handle this herself, but she wasn't alone. "It's okay to feel awful, but remember God hasn't given you anything more than you can handle." She didn't need a sermon, not from him, he knew that much. But he'd been down this sorry road and he could help her.

"I just don't know what I did to deserve this."

"You did nothing."

She looked at him with watery eyes glistening in the security lights that filled the compound. "Then why all this heartache, if I'm not being punished for anything?"

"People think that bad things are a result of divine punishment. It's an old argument." He smiled softly, and was rewarded with an intense stare. "I told you the other morning that I'm studying Job," he said.

"Yes. God allowed terrible things to happen to him. Job suffered. Then Christ suffered. I know all that."

"God's ways are not our ways. He values our faith and trust in Him more than anything." Hunter paused. "And all we have to do is trust that He knows what's best for us."

"Is that why you accepted your prison term so easily?"

For a fleeting moment, Hunter wondered how much she knew of the truth. "The price has been paid."

"My father has done something terrible, hasn't he? Or else we wouldn't be fighting for our lives. But he always thought of me as a baby, someone to protect. He had a lot of pride."

"If we continue to seek God and not curse Him, He will take care of us."

She nodded, but Hunter knew she was nearing the breaking point.

The urge to come clean with her almost swamped him. Like before, he knew he had no right to burden her further with the truth about her father. But what right did Benton have now, after his death, to force Hunter to keep up the charade?

He should say something. "Do up your seat belt," he ordered tightly.

■ ■ ■ ■

Rae gripped the dash. Confusion swirled within her. Her father had warned Hunter about some danger and, thinking of her as that little motherless child of years ago, hadn't told Rae herself.

What had Dad been involved in? Had he been blackmailed for some reason, forced to do something he didn't want to do?

Cutter Stevenson's words echoed back to her. He believed Dad and Hunter were involved in something illegal. Then Hunter had asked her to trust him, and more importantly, trust God.

A part of her ached to pull Hunter close and try to somehow forget all that had happened, even for a few minutes.

Rae forced the warring emotions from her mind. She fought the urge to ask Hunter for the truth, once and for all. He needed to concentrate on the slick road. . . .

With the village of Green Valley behind them, Rae noticed Hunter had decided to stick to the main highway instead of the shortcut through a new subdivision she often took. It would add time and miles to the trip, but she wasn't about to complain. She needed the time to think.

Was this God's plan? If they arrived too soon back at her workshop, she might give in and demand the truth from him. Maybe it was best to let it go for the night. It would give her time to pray about it.

They crossed a small bridge at the edge of the village, and eventually, leaving the houses behind, followed a lonely, twisting road up the hillside.

The rain had begun again. Another set of headlights appeared behind them, and Rae bit her lip. That vehicle was traveling too fast for the slippery conditions.

The car sped toward them, slowing at the last possible minute.

Hunter grimaced. "Crazy driver."

She looked behind them. The vehicle pulled back a bit, putting some space between them. Then, with no warning, the driver hit the gas again, roaring up close. "Let him pass," she muttered. "They'll pull him out of the ditch in the morning."

The road curved to the left, and just as Hunter began to turn in that direction, a loud thunk rocked the truck, and both of them were jerked back against the seat. Hunter glared into the rearview mirror. "He's ramming us!"

"Pull over!"

Hunter hit the brake. He said something

she didn't catch, and glanced down at his foot as he pumped it repeatedly. "The brakes aren't working!"

Another brutal thump rocked the truck as Hunter tried to steer off the road, but the slick pavement and the angry driver behind them had other plans.

They skidded, and the next blow slammed them against the guardrail between the road and the gorge beyond. For several horrible seconds they scraped along the metal barrier. Rae twisted around to stare out the back window. The vehicle behind them gave one last heave forward.

She screamed.

"Hang on!" Hunter's right foot still hard on the foot pedal, he grabbed the emergency brake. At the same time, he steered the truck perpendicular to the slope and jammed the gearshift into Park.

The transmission protested with a sickening grinding sound, but the truck didn't stop.

They plunged into the deep ravine.

TWELVE

Hunter awoke to find both of them pinned by their seat belts. The old truck had no air bags, so he had a clear view of the windshield. Several trees had caught them. Ahead, lit by the dying headlights, was the bottom of the ravine.

"Rae?"

She stirred beside him.

"Rae! Wake up, talk to me!" Ignoring the pain in his chest, he braced himself against the steering wheel and pushed back, giving the seat belt enough slack for him to undo it. With his knees raised, he shifted around to face her. Rae's head had obviously smacked against the dash. She reached up to touch her forehead, and he could see her wince. Deciding to get out and crawl over the back window to get her, he tried to throw open his door. It wouldn't budge.

He turned back to Rae, "Where are you hurt?"

"Just my head," she whispered. "Are you all right?"

"I'm okay."

"Thank goodness you weren't going too fast."

His heart pounding with relief, he nodded. He would expect such a moment as this to crawl by in slow, painful increments, but the whole thing seemed a blur, followed by the horror of thinking that Rae might be killed.

He reached down and shut off the ignition. Then he doused the headlights. Rae reached across the dark space between them, finding his hand and squeezing it hard.

"We're alive." She sighed. "And even though my prayers lately haven't been so nice and thankful, I think we should thank God. Right now."

Warmth surged through him. Yes, she loved the Lord, but as she said, lately she'd been fighting what was happening to her. A modern-day Job. Asking for a prayer of thanksgiving gave her credit, and he felt his heart swell.

He grasped her fingers and shut his eyes. "Thank You, Lord, for getting us through this safely. We don't know Your will here, but we know You care for us. Help us to learn to trust You more."

They both said *amen.*

Rae disconnected her hand from his. "Did you see what kind of car rammed us?"

"A truck, that's all. Forget him for now. Let's get out of here. Can you manage?"

She nodded, and pushed herself back to loosen the seat belt. He unsnapped it. With a thud, she fell forward and groaned. "I'm okay. Just weak."

As soon as she unlatched the door, it fell open with a screech. "Easy now," he warned as she dropped to the sloping wall of the ravine. Wincing at the ache in his chest, he climbed out behind her. A wet branch slapped his head. Above, the wind loosened rainwater from the few leaves left on the trees, and the cold drops showered down on them.

"I have a flashlight somewhere behind the seat," she said as she grabbed her knapsack out of the truck.

He found that it had rolled up under the dash. He dug it out, noticing that the brake pedal had flopped to the fire wall between the cab and the engine.

He straightened. "The brakes are shot."

"I noticed that. Bad timing, don't you think?" The sarcasm in her voice told him she didn't believe it to be a coincidence.

"Let's get up to the road. We'll see if we can flag someone down."

"Wait."

He grasped her arm as they leaned precariously against the truck. Holding his breath, he listened. Someone was driving slowly along the road.

"Down the ravine," he growled, shoving her forward. They twisted around the open door and plunged down the steep incline.

"This way." Flicking off the flashlight, he pointed to their left, in the opposite direction from the approaching vehicle. Once, Rae tripped and let out a sharp cry. Hunter scooped her up and threw her over his shoulder, all the while plowing downward through the thick growth of forest. Branches of all sizes resisted their flight, but he ignored them.

At some point, he stepped into a stream, running fast and cold due to the recent rains. He slipped, and was forced to set Rae down. Near a small waterfall, they crouched and peered back at the truck.

Above, the headlights of a large car or truck cut a wide swath through the tops of the trees. They heard a door slam and then someone with a powerful flashlight scanned the crash site, arcing the beam dangerously close to their heads. Rae clung to Hunter, and he felt her quickening breath against his shoulder. Ahead, by the truck, a rustling noise sounded.

Abruptly, a gun fired, its golden flash and harsh report startling them. They heard a scurrying sound, and Hunter tucked Rae against his chest, afraid she'd cry out. Someone wanted them dead, all right, and running them off the road wasn't enough.

Hunter didn't dare move. They were so close to the small waterfall that he could feel the cold water seeping into his clothes. The smell of rotting forest leaves surrounded them.

Rae shifted, and he tugged her closer.

They waited, barely breathing, as the shooter searched the area near the truck. Whoever it was slipped once in the soft earth of the ravine, and Hunter heard the man's muttered curse. He didn't recognize the voice.

The shooter slipped again. In the flashlight beam Hunter caught a glimpse of dark clothing and a male frame, but nothing more.

Finally, the man struggled up the slope to the road.

"Someone doesn't like us," Rae whispered.

"And we're not hanging around to find

out why. Come on."

Grabbing her hand, Hunter led her farther downstream, this time with much more care, all the while praying that the sounds of the rushing water would drown out their footfalls. They worked their way to the bottom of the hill. Thoroughly tired, and what seemed like hours later, Hunter noticed that the cold stream was now calf-deep and racing past them. And that his feet were numb.

Rae slipped again, splashing into the water with a small cry. He lifted her onto the bank, then crawled up beside her. When she started shivering, he peeled off his coat and wrapped it around her. It was damp, but better than the thin jacket she wore.

In the dark, he heard her sniff. "Hold me, Hunter," she whispered. "Hold me tight."

He obliged, pulling her against his chest and burying his face in her wet hair. The rain had released her lingering rose scent, mixing it with the earthy smell of the autumn forest. She smelled wonderful.

They clung to each other. The incident of the shavings in the shop's woodstove seemed mild compared to what had just happened. Whoever it was, he was getting serious.

No way was Hunter going to let that someone succeed.

He felt Rae lift her head. "Thank you,

Hunter. I don't know what I would have done without you."

Even in the dark, he knew where to find her mouth. She clung to his shoulders and returned his kiss.

I believe Rae is in danger. You've got to help us.

Benton's words crashed into his mind like the stream crashed into the rocks that lined the riverbed.

Hunter peeled her away from him, clenching his jaw to stop from kissing her again. "We should get onto the road."

"I agree, but where are we?"

"I'd say we're just outside of Riverview. I can hear some traffic ahead."

"Do you think we've traveled that far?"

He nodded. They climbed out of the ravine and found themselves at the edge of a new subdivision, in a new backyard. Through the trees, he spied a low-flying passenger jet preparing to land at the Moncton airport. Its trajectory told him they had to be close to the river that separated the cities.

"Let's find a phone," she suggested. "Call the police and a taxi."

"We're not going home or reporting this, not yet."

"Why not?"

"Rae, someone tried to burn down your shop, blow up your house, then smother you, and he's not only run you off the road, but also climbed down to finish the job with a high-powered firearm. Something the police carry. We're going to a hotel in the city."

"A hotel! Hunter, I have no money."

"Don't worry. You'll — we'll be fine. Have faith."

She wet her lips. He knew she wanted to voice the question of how he knew they'd be fine, but his comment on faith stopped her. It wasn't fair to put her in such a position when all he would have to do was be honest with her. It felt like he was criticizing her faith and then testing it.

"We can't hide, Hunter. The police need to know what happened."

"The brakes died, someone in a truck ran us off the road, then with a very powerful, heavy-duty flashlight, tried to locate us to finish us off. The police often carry high-powered rifles with them, in case they have to put down deer or moose that have been hit by cars."

"So?"

"Who had access to your truck last? Who would own a big, tough flashlight and have access to a large vehicle?"

She stared at him, wide-eyed and blinking in disbelief.

"I'm not saying that Halloway is trying to kill us. All I'm saying is that I won't take any chances with your life. Now, we need a safe place to spend the night."

"Annie's?"

"Back to Green Valley? Not a good idea."

Rae began to protest again, but when a car drove past the half-built house, she stopped. They froze until the vehicle was again out of sight. "All right. Let's go then."

They walked, cold and numb, to a small gas station at the end of the road, where they called a taxi. Once inside, Hunter ordered the cabbie to drive them across the river to one of Moncton's best hotels.

Twenty minutes later, they arrived. "I doubt anyone would think we've come here," he told her as they watched the taxi pull away from the lobby door. Behind them was affluence neither of them was used to. Only important people stayed here, including the queen of England herself, a few years back.

Rae brushed herself off as they walked inside. "I just hope we don't stand out too much."

Hunter spoke quietly with the man at the desk. Keeping one eye on Rae, who stood facing the discreet, tasteful courtyard, he quickly registered, using most of the cash he had to book two rooms.

Within minutes, they found hers, and then Hunter's across the hall.

"How can we be sure we won't be found?" she asked as she stepped over the threshold of her room.

"Money buys a certain amount of discretion. Go take a bath," he ordered. "I have a few phone calls to make."

Rae nodded. At the door to the decadent bathroom, she glanced back. He caught her studying him as he turned to go. "What's wrong?"

She smiled. "Nothing. Despite your filthy outfit, you kind of look like you belong here."

Yeah, right. He was an ex-con with a troubled childhood. He was scarred, and the decade of incarceration had etched deep lines on his face. She was just seeing him taking charge of the situation.

Lord, help me do the right things.

"Go take your bath, Rae." He closed the door and headed into his own room.

When he heard his door shut tight behind him, he hung his head. Would this have happened if he and Benton hadn't broken the law ten years ago? What danger had they dragged Rae into? What was he doing now? Her growing compassion for him made him weak and unfocused, the worst thing to be right now.

His heart clenched. Could he even take a chance on love? He was too caught up in his own failings, the stigma of being an ex-con and the fear of opening up his heart as he had to others who'd deserted him.

Shaking his head, he did what he'd always done: kept going. He yanked a business card from his jacket pocket and stabbed out the number. He needed some answers.

Rae couldn't deal with a bath right now. She was simply too keyed up. Hunter was across the hall, and sometime during this last day, her distrust of him had melted away.

Her father would be proud of her. While the notion warmed her, it came with a grief she'd become sick of. Yes, she trusted Hunter. But as long as he was here, he'd remind her that all he'd done had resulted in her father's death.

Yet trust had its merits, too, didn't it? She rinsed her face and hair, then finger-combed the messy locks, grateful for the warmth around her. Yes, she needed to trust some-one.

Despite the cheerful room, she shivered. Who was to say that the shooter in the woods was after her? Hunter had been the target of retaliation in prison. Could someone still in prison have ordered a hit on him?

She quickly dried her face. Then, after checking her bedraggled appearance one last time, she headed to his room.

Hunter threw open the door, his expression dark.

"No bath?"

"Too keyed up." She stalked in. "Look, Hunter, how do we know these attacks are directed at me? Could someone in prison with you be retaliating against you for some reason?"

"This isn't about me. One of the guys who shanked me is dead, and the other has been moved to maximum security. No one else cared."

Rae bit her lip. She'd already decided she trusted him. She *wanted* to trust him. She began to speak, but Hunter shook his head. "Let me have a quick shower before we go any further. Go back to your room."

Nodding, she turned, catching a glimpse of several sheets of the hotel's notepaper beside the phone. He had a pen in his hand, and obviously, he'd scribbled down something she couldn't quite read. An address?

When she returned to her room, her stomach growled. She headed for the basket of complimentary snacks, and chose some nuts and fruit and bottled juice. All the while, her mind was whirring.

Just as she finished them off, Hunter knocked on the door.

"Okay," she said as she let him in, "before we start trying to figure out why anyone would wish me dead, I want to say something."

"About what?"

"The money. You paid for the room with cash and I know I've asked you about it —"

"I'll explain about the money later."

"Then tell me what my father was doing that has got us into this mess! Was it something you two did ten years ago?"

"I don't know for sure."

With gritted teeth she sank onto one of the Queen Anne style chairs in the corner. Here she was, trying to be open and honest with him, but he was still holding back. Had his childhood caused such mistrust? Or his time in prison?

"It's okay," she said, partly to herself. "I'm sorry if I was pressuring you to tell me things that are none of my business. But let me say this. I trust you, Hunter. So you should trust me."

He looked away. "It's not that easy. You have no idea."

"Then tell me."

Emotions she couldn't identify warred in his eyes. What was it that he couldn't tell her? Was it really about her father? But what had Robert Benton done that Hunter would so determinedly keep silent about?

Without warning, the phone rang, a jarring electronic sound that cut through her. She jumped.

Hunter paused, and she knew that he, too, was unnerved by its interruption.

At the third ring, he reached for it.

For a breathless minute, he listened. His deepening frown and tight lips made her heart sink. Something was wrong.

Then he pinned her with a sharp look. "We have to get out of here. Now!"

THIRTEEN

Hunter dropped the phone onto its cradle with a clatter. Rae stepped back. "What's going on? Who was on the phone?"

"I'll tell you later." He glanced sharply around for anything they might forget. "Let's go."

"Where are we going?"

He grabbed her hand, allowing her to scoop up her knapsack-style purse before they raced down the hall. When they reached the corner, he scanned the empty corridor with a feeling of relief.

"We've got to take the stairs. It's too easy for him to come up the elevator."

She gasped. "Who? Our shooter?"

"My guess. But I'm not going to test it."

To their right, the elevator dinged. Still gripping Rae's wrist, Hunter hurried down the stairwell. Thankfully, she had no trouble keeping up.

A sharp ping ricocheted off the wall beside

them, and Hunter shoved Rae down to the tiled floor of the landing. Above them, hurried footfalls followed.

They both jumped up. Hunter pushed Rae forward and she rushed down the rest of the stairs, with him close on her heels. When they reached the ground floor, both panting, he barreled through the fire escape door and dragged her outside.

The back of the building faced the Petitcodiac River, and the lights of Riverview twinkling beyond. Hunter glanced both ways. Since the hotel connected with several other buildings in the downtown core, they were forced to circumvent the whole long block.

Another shot rang out, hitting the corner bricks and sending chips flying. One hit Hunter's face, and he swiped at his stinging cheek. "Run!"

Reaching Main Street, they turned right and sprinted back toward the hotel. The complex of buildings was preferable to the open parking lot on the other side.

Hunter didn't expect to find a taxi cruising around, but when they reached the front courtyard less than a minute later, he spied one. He pushed Rae into the cab behind the driver, swiftly circling the back of the vehicle to climb in himself.

"Top of Mountain Road," he panted. "Magnetic Hill. Hurry!"

The driver nodded and sped away. Peering behind them, out the back window, Hunter saw no one suspicious. In the distance, police sirens wailed.

Magnetic Hill, the city's most famous tourist site, was at the opposite end of town, and would take nearly fifteen minutes to reach. It would give him time to explain things to Rae.

"What's going on?" she asked as the vehicle careened around a corner.

"I paid the night manager to tip me off if someone came in asking for us. He's not supposed to give out room numbers, but he's got a trainee working with him tonight who accidentally fell for the guy's line. I doubt that she'll have a job come tomorrow."

"Did she get a description?"

"Probably. I'll find out later."

Rae leaned forward. "How did whoever was shooting at us even know where we were?"

"My guess is that he figured that we'd head down the ravine toward Riverview. Then, we'd need a safe hotel in the area. That hotel was the best, so he probably started there, and bingo, we were checked in."

"Shouldn't we go back to talk to the police? They'll want to interview us."

"Remember who might have run us off the road."

She swallowed. "So why are we going to Magnetic Hill?"

"I have an acquaintance who lives up there."

"Who?"

"A cellmate who was an investor and whose biggest mistake was ripping off clients who could afford good lawyers. He's out now and back home in Moncton."

"And he'll appreciate us just dropping by?"

Hunter took her hand and squeezed it. Louis Carriere had been amiable enough to once tell Hunter he could stop by anytime. He'd called the old man tonight for some information that he knew Louis would be able to get quietly. The man had reiterated his invitation to visit him.

"How well do you know this guy?"

"Louis is a good man, Rae. At least now he is. He gave his life to Christ while he was in prison. He's pragmatic, too, which actually helped with his incarceration."

"How?"

"He knew he'd get caught sooner or later, and was quite willing to do his time. In prison, he was even recommended for the minimum-security area, but turned it down. We were friends by then, and he wanted to learn more about Jesus from me."

"Did you lead him to the Lord?"

"In a way. Louis had grown up in a very traditional and conservative church and family. He knew all about Jesus, but had no relationship with Him until I explained mine."

Rae nodded. "I understand. For me, it was in high school, when I was at my most awkward, that I learned how much God loves me. But will this guy really help us?"

"I think that Louis wants to somehow make up for his criminal ways."

Homes and businesses whisked by as the pair settled into a tense, nervous silence. To ease it, Hunter lifted Rae's right hand and kissed it. She grabbed his other hand and scooted closer to him. "Are we going to be safe at this guy's house?" she whispered.

"I'll make sure of it."

The taxi turned onto Mountain Road, a street that sliced through Moncton. Restaurants, nightclubs and an assortment of other shops and services lined its long length.

Five minutes later, Hunter ordered the

cabbie to stop at a gas station at the base of Magnetic Hill. After he paid, he helped Rae out. Up here, the wind had free rein and blew through him. He noticed Rae shivering, and led her toward the station as the cab disappeared back down Mountain Road.

Turning sharply, he took Rae's hand. "Are you up for a walk?"

"Definitely. I feel gross in these dirty clothes, but I can walk as far as you can."

Squeezing her fingers, he smiled. "Good."

Hunter hurried them past the entrance to the tourist area. Though closed up for the winter, the quaint shops, covered bridge and zoo no doubt had surveillance cameras. No, it was better to walk the long way around.

It took them nearly an hour to reach a spacious home on the top of the mountain.

Hunter heard Rae's soft panting as they approached it. "What's this guy's name?"

"Louis Carriere. He did time for an investment scam a few years back."

Rae looked around the grand front entrance. "The police didn't get all the money back, I'm guessing."

Hunter laughed softly as he rang the doorbell. "Louis was already wealthy. He's quite an investor. Good nose for things like that. He also has his nose in everything going on in the area."

"And you think he'll know why someone wants me dead? How's that possible?"

Hunter wasn't sure, and was just hoping it might be true. "I think land is at the center of this, but I don't know anything more. Louis dabbled in development for a while."

"How do know it's about land?"

"Think about it, Rae. It's what connects all the people we suspect."

"But not Constable Halloway. He's just a police officer."

At that moment, a wiry, gray-haired man opened the door.

"Louis."

"Hunter! I'm glad you made it here. I was getting concerned." He looked curiously at Rae, and Hunter quickly introduced them, using only her first name. The man tipped his head and smiled warmly. "My pleasure," he said with a smooth, but thick French accent. "Come in. Don't stand out there in the cold."

"Thanks," Hunter answered. The old Frenchman had shrugged off his prison sentence and done his time, learning from the Bible and quietly writing his memoirs, a thing he'd been meaning to complete for years, he'd often said.

Louis shut the door. "How are you doing? I hear you have inherited a potful of money and a good business."

Hunter tossed a sharp look at Rae, who, thankfully, was staring in awe at an Italian marble floor and the grandest staircase in Moncton. He looked back at Louis. "Where did you hear that?"

"I keep in touch with the right people."

Hunter lifted his eyebrows. "One of the ways you acquired information was illegal. Didn't you pay people to spy for information?"

The older man smiled. "The Lord has shown me how wrong my life was before. Still, old contacts offer information freely, and I accept it."

As he spoke, the man took their jackets to hang them up. Rae continued to gape at the immaculate entrance. Hunter had never been here, either, but quelled his curiosity in favor of safety.

The niceties done with, their host said, "I know this isn't just a social call, not after what you said on the phone."

"Unfortunately, no. But first, thank you for seeing us."

"No thanks needed. I owe you my life, my friend. You did so much for me, even when you were concerned for your friend's safety."

Rae grew alert. She looked at Hunter when he answered, "Yes, I remember."

Louis smiled at her. "Let's have coffee. It will warm you up." He ushered them into his living room at the back of the house.

A stretch of wide windows offered a panorama of the city below. Even in the dark, wet night, the view was stunning.

Rae cleared her throat a bit timidly. "Before we talk, you wouldn't have anything I could change into? Perhaps your wife . . . ?"

"She left me years ago. *Mais oui,* you both should change. I've got some things that may fit."

He led them to a large bedroom that had the same view of Moncton. Both Hunter and Rae took in the space with awe. A wide bed occupied nearly the entire left wall. To the right, a gas fireplace took center stage, flanked by wing chairs. Beside the door stood an antique armoire, and a door beyond the bed led to the en suite bathroom. The whole ambience spoke of old-world charm and great expense. Louis might be a criminal, but he was incredibly civilized.

Hunter and Louis left, returning a moment later with their arms laden with clothes, which they dropped on the bed. Rae rummaged through the soft, clean garments until she found a pair of fleece pants and a matching sweater. "Louis, how could your wife leave all these?" she asked.

Hunter grinned. "A piece of advice — don't ask him. He's liable to tell you the truth. All that matters is they're clean and dry."

"Yes." If nothing else, Rae was practical, not the sort who'd balk at wearing other people's clothes. Of course, what they'd gone through lately would change even the most uncompromising mind.

"Hunter?"

He'd been following their host out the bedroom door, but stopped, and when he turned, the cautious hope in his eyes made her cringe. The memory of their kiss still lingered between them.

"What's happening? Tell me your suspicions. What was so terrible that my father couldn't say anything? We've gone from burying Dad to running for our lives, not once, but twice. Now we're standing in the spare bedroom of an ex-con I didn't know existed." She shook her head, exasperated and confused. "You've got to trust me to help, too, and not think you have to protect me."

Hunter gripped the clothes the older man

had found for him. "When I called Louis, I had some ideas on where to look if we're to find someone who would benefit from your death. He'll help."

"What if it's you they're after?"

She watched as his lips drew into a thin, tight line. Finally, he said, "If we discover it's me they want, I'll leave, and you'll be safe."

"*Would* I be safe?"

"I'd make sure of it."

She didn't want him to leave. Days ago, she hadn't wanted him to step onto her property, but somewhere between the two moments in time, she'd found she could forgive him for what he'd done. He wasn't the same troubled kid who'd entered prison.

Still, she asked, "*Shouldn't* we call the police? If Halloway tampered with my brakes, other police could protect us, couldn't they?"

"Yes, but we'd need a lot more proof than what we have."

"You don't trust them, do you?"

"It's not that. I want you safe. I made a promise to your father. Get changed before you get sick."

She ignored the clothes piled on the neatly made bed. "Hunter, I'm not a child. I've buried both my parents. I've given my life

181

to the Lord. I may not be perfect, but I can handle more than you think I can."

His expression softened just before he turned and left.

Lord, give me strength to accept whatever has happened, she prayed.

Fifteen minutes later, they were downstairs in the living room, decaf coffee in hand.

Louis handed her a plate of thick, soft molasses cookies. Rae ate one, trying not to appear as hungry as she felt. Hunter polished the rest of them off.

They sat together on the suede sofa. Louis took a nearby easy chair, a debonair man with finesse and confidence. In fact, his face glowed with a peace only strong faith could provide.

"So when did you get this place?" Hunter asked.

"I had it built before I went to prison. I owned most of the land up here and subdivided it off. With the money, I built my castle. Now, knowing the Lord wants me to serve Him, I'm thinking of selling it and giving the money back to Him."

"It's too bad your wife didn't stick around long enough to enjoy this." Though Hunter's tone was light, Rae could hear an underlying edge to it. She knew why. All of the people he'd loved had, at some time, deserted him.

The old man laughed. "*Non!* My wife left me at the first sign of trouble, years ago. When she heard I'd sold part of this land, she tried to take what she felt was her share of the money, but it didn't happen. I'd owned it before she came along."

He sipped his coffee, an indecipherable expression on his face. When he set down his mug, he smiled. "So, Hunter, how did you end up with this beauty?"

Rae flushed. She wasn't beautiful. She was plain, her only attribute being that she was neat and clean. Most of the time, anyway.

Hunter set down his own coffee. "She's Robert Benton's daughter."

Louis threw up his eyebrows, obviously surprised. Then, just as quickly, he added, "*Pardon, ma chère.* But all those times Benton visited —"

Gaping, Rae flicked her gaze back and forth between the men. Louis again apologized in French. And right then, Rae knew if she was going to get to the bottom of things, she'd have to accept the whole ugly truth, including how her father trusted Hunter more than he trusted her.

FOURTEEN

Rae's heart pounded. Was she ready to hear everything? She looked at Louis, who was peering at her cautiously. "How long were you in prison?"

"Three years."

"When?"

Louis looked over to Hunter before answering. "At the end of Hunter's sentence. I was released on parole a few months ago. However, Hunter served a full term, so he doesn't have to report to anyone."

She blinked at Hunter. "For at least three years, Dad visited you? What did he tell you?"

Hunter stood, looking past her to speak to their host. "Could you excuse us for a moment, Louis?"

With a nod, the old man gathered up the mugs and disappeared into the kitchen.

Rae's mouth felt dry. "Hunter, you've been evasive enough. Don't you think I deserve to know? Don't you think I can handle this?"

He said nothing. She waited, her gaze locked to his. Brilliant clear eyes met hers, and she hated the conflict in them. She stood and walked to the wide, panoramic window. "I deserve to know. We both agree on that. I can see it in your eyes. Tell me the truth, Hunter."

"Don't you think there's a good reason for me not to tell you what I know?"

"Then tell me why he believed he had to visit you. Why did he feel he had to see you and keep me in the dark about his illness? Because he felt responsible for you?"

Hunter walked toward the window in turn, stopping to stare out. "He considered himself my mentor. He didn't want me to end up a career criminal, or back on the streets where he'd found me. And yes, he told me he had cancer, but he never meant any of this to hurt you, Rae." Hunter drew in a deep breath. "I was the one who led him to the Lord. I gave him some books to read, and he listened when I told me what had happened in my life, how I could forgive him —" Hunter stopped abruptly. "I mean, I was a mixed up kid, getting mad at the world for no reason."

Rae shut her eyes. She remembered the

day Dad had told her he was going to church with her. That Sunday service, she'd seen him cry during the worship music. Thin and sickly, and still attributing his bad health to a cold, he had told her he finally accepted Jesus into his heart.

Tears sprang into her eyes as the memory cut through her. She dipped her head to touch the cool glass in front of her. "How did he meet you? I don't remember."

"I was hanging around local coffee shops and getting into fights. I'd dropped out of school and knew nothing but anger. One day, he paid me to load up the truck, and then did so again, and again. I was rough and crude and trying to be bigger than I was. Once, he saw I'd been in a fight. He took me to the hospital, they cleaned me up and he took me to your house."

"I remember that. I came home from school and you were sitting in the workshop with an ice pack."

"He cared for me, but he always said he would protect you, even from me, if necessary."

She offered up a weak smile. "That explains why you slept in the workshop that night."

He smiled back. "You were fifteen and couldn't be bothered with me."

"Not true. I noticed you. You were a way cool eighteen-year-old."

"I didn't know that." He shook his head. "It wouldn't have mattered. I had too much respect for your father to pull any stunts with his daughter. Besides, you always had your friends around."

"Not too many left anymore. Everyone's moved away, except Annie. She stayed in Green Valley, married Kirk, who was a local himself." She paused, then asked, "How often did Dad visit? What did you talk about?"

"I didn't want to see him at first. Then, after I'd accepted the Lord, it got easier. I finally . . ." Hunter stopped, then took a hesitant step forward. "Rae, your father wasn't perfect. But I'm thankful he came to visit me. He was the only one who ever did. I don't want this to upset you, but you asked."

He'd been saved and had showed her father the Lord. How could she be upset over that? Rae straightened, and her heart squeezed as she realized that Hunter's voice had dropped into a quiet, pained tone. How lonely it must have been for him. She rubbed her arms. "And your family?"

"I have no idea where my mother is. She walked out on me numerous times when I was young. That's how I ended up in foster homes. Then she'd always come back to get me, until she couldn't be bothered anymore. When I turned sixteen, she dropped by the apartment we were supposed to have rented for a year, to say that we'd been evicted and she was leaving. Going to Montreal or Toronto or someplace. She said she'd call when she got settled. She never did."

"And your dad? Your brother?"

"I never knew either, and I only found out I had an older brother just before my mother left the last time. He probably doesn't even know I exist. That's the way it is sometimes, Rae. You take what you get for family." Hunter pulled her down to the couch, and lifted his hand to stroke her cheek. Tears had welled in her eyes and she blinked them back, only to find more welling up. In the distance, Louis's phone rang.

Hunter brushed her tears away. "Don't ask me any more about it, Rae. Just forgive your dad and me. We have other, more important things that need to be dealt with."

She nodded, and through the blur of tears, noticed strong relief wash over his features.

A sudden yawn rippled through her and she tried to suppress it. Hunter stood, took her hand and pulled her up. "Come on, you're beat. Off to bed."

"No, I should stay up, too. This is about me."

"There may not be anything to stay up for."

In the light from the chandelier high above, she could see the ridge of scar along Hunter's cheek. The prison souvenir threw back at her all that her father had kept from her, but had told Hunter.

No, this wasn't fair. Her father *wasn't* perfect. There was a good chance he'd been involved in something deadly. Rae cringed inwardly at the thought as they headed for Louis's study. Whatever his reasons, her dad should have thought of her.

In a small study off the front foyer, Louis was busy scribbling down some notes. With its dark wood and rich leather, the room had everything an investor might want in a private office. Their host looked grim when he lifted his head. Rae's stomach tightened.

"What did you find out?" she asked.

"How well do you know this man?" He turned his computer screen around. It showed a newspaper article with a picture of Cutter Stevenson walking up the stairs of a courthouse in handcuffs. While his hair was thicker and darker, he was definitely recognizable.

Her mouth open, Rae leaned forward.

"That's Cutter! I only met him the other day, but he knew my father. What was he arrested for?"

"Which time? I just found out he was arrested this afternoon for threatening the public with a firearm. But when this article was written, he was arrested for illegally logging on crown land. Even though it's public land, the government doesn't allow logging unless you have a permit. Cutter Stevenson was logging small amounts, but it was what he was logging that got him caught."

Rae glanced up at Hunter, who spoke. "Bird's-eye maple, right? And he had a knack for guessing which tree had that pattern, correct?"

Louis nodded. "Just by looking at the bark, he claims. He had a good success rate, according to the trial transcripts."

"And because," Hunter added, scanning the article, "this kind of wood fetches up to seventy dollars a linear foot, it's lucrative for a man with his own portable mill. But a private investigation by a big logging company matched the wood to the stumps. And they turned over their findings to the police."

"However," Louis stated, "I've learned that there was legal logging allowed in that area, too, to clear the land for a big development."

Rae sank down in one of the leather chairs opposite the desk and looked at Hunter. "What did Cutter say about Dad? Something about doing his dirty work, and that he should have been paid for it, but wasn't?"

Hunter's mouth was set as tight as his jaw. She turned to Louis, who was now searching other Web sites. "There's more," he said. "You know Andy Morrison?"

Rae gasped. "They've found him? Is he dead?"

Louis shook his head patiently. "*Non.* He is still missing, but with good reason. I have a source who says that Andy Morrison is under investigation for selling government land."

"Is that illegal? I mean, part of his job is to arrange for leases and such."

"If the government wants to sell its own land, it has a right to do so, but it's rarely done and only through public tender," Louis said, tapping his keyboard all the while.

"What he means is Morrison is suspected of selling land that hasn't been approved for sale," Hunter interjected. "It's suspected that he's been forging the paperwork and letting it go for rock-bottom prices."

"That doesn't make sense. If you're going to sell land, wouldn't you want to make as much money as you can?"

"I doubt he's selling it to himself," Louis said after reading one site on credit ratings. "He has very poor credit and no cash. And if he couldn't pay cash, he'd have to get a mortgage, and that mortgage would have to be registered at the very place he works."

"How can he get away with that? Surely it would have to go through a thousand government channels first."

"The land registry system has changed in recent years. It's all electronic now, and it was Morrison's job to convert it over. The old registry books will be kept because they are now historical documents. But they'll be set aside and not consulted after all the information is put into the computer."

"So you're thinking that Andy entered false information into the database, then did something with the registry books so that it can't be confirmed?" She looked at both men. "Or did he falsify the old books? It may not be hard to rewrite a page or two to the way he wants them to read."

"I think there are many ways he could cheat the system, and those are two of them," Louis stated.

"But," Louis added, "it's where the land

is that's interesting. Some government property would be hard to sell because of its location. But if it's in the middle of a forest, or alongside rural acreage that is rarely visited, it may not be so noticeable."

Rae leaned back in the chair. "Don't tell me. It's very close to mine, right? I know there's been some logging near my house."

With a yawn, Louis shut down his computer and turned off the monitor. *We're all tired,* Rae thought. Though how she was going to sleep was beyond her. Had her dad been involved with the illegal logging or purchase of land? She bit her lip, focusing on the floor while she thought. If her father had been a part of either or both, of course he wouldn't tell her. He'd be afraid she'd do the Christian thing.

Would she have? She couldn't answer that, not tonight.

She leaned across the desk toward Louis. "Thank you so much. We'd have taken much longer to figure this out by ourselves."

He dipped his head in acknowledgement. "My small way to give back, after years of taking." His smile failed. "But remember, even the illegal harvest of trees from public land is a dangerous business now."

Hunter also went grim. "What he means is, people are willing to kill over it."

■ ■ ■ ■

The birth of a new day glowed through the wide windows downstairs. The view included the mottled forest and wide stretch of city Hunter had admired last night, and he found his spirits lifting.

Louis had laid out juice, coffee and tea, complete with cream and sugar, all arranged neatly on a lace covered table.

Now if only Rae would appear.

But after last night, before they'd discovered Stevenson's tree theft, and Morrison's alleged misappropriation of government land, Hunter had opened up a bit to her about Benton's visits to him. Had easing his own burden added to hers? Yet he couldn't lie to her, and he'd hoped to show her father's compassion.

He sat down and poured a cup of coffee. The slanting sun beat in on him, strong for the cool, fall day. He could hear Louis puttering around in the kitchen. The old man was glad for the company, he could tell, and Hunter was glad they'd come here. He lifted his mug to his lips.

Rae came to the doorway of the breakfast nook. "Good morning."

Hunter's heart leaped. "Good morning."

She slipped into a seat beside him. "Sleep well?"

"Lousy. I was mad at myself for upsetting you."

She touched his hand. "I thought about it. If I had no one to visit me in jail, I wouldn't have discouraged the only person who came. It's still hard to think that Dad is gone and that he wasn't perfect, but you're right. He would have done anything to make sure I was okay. Whatever I learn about him, I'll have to remember that."

Hunter smiled. It was easy for her to say that now, but if she found out everything, would she be so accommodating? Her father had burned down his own workshop to destroy evidence that he and Hunter had been stealing rare wood. Though Hunter had never met Cutter Stevenson until this week, he knew now that he was the third party involved in their business.

"Good morning, you two!" Louis trotted out of the kitchen carrying a steaming tray of sausages, croissants and scrambled eggs. The old man wore a fancy, feminine pink apron, bringing a smile to Hunter's face. Beside him, Rae giggled.

Louis plucked at the apron. "A souvenir from my ex-wife. Though I don't ever remember her wearing it. She never cooked.

Perhaps I should leave it in the house when I sell it."

"Good idea," Hunter answered. "It's not your color."

Chuckling, Louis set the tray in the center of the table. "I did a bit of research early this morning, and discovered a few interesting points."

Hunter stopped with his mug halfway to his mouth. Wide-eyed, Rae stared at the older man.

He offered Rae a plate. "Help yourself while it's hot."

"What did you find out? Who's trying to kill me?"

"Eat. It's only good when it's fresh."

Obviously frustrated, Rae forked up a sausage and snatched a croissant. "Well?"

The old man continued, directing his words to her. "What do you know about Hilltop Settlement?"

She shook her head. "Nothing. Is it a village near here?"

Louis chuckled. "*Non.* How far is your house from the highway?"

"Driving? Less than fifteen minutes." Her expression reflected Hunter's own confusion. "I have to go through town to reach it."

"As the crow flies?"

She shrugged. "Less than a kilometer. On hot summer nights, I can hear the trucks go by."

Hunter took the plate Louis offered him. "Why do you ask?"

"And if you clear-cut your land? What kind of view would you have?"

"You'd be able to see all of southeast New Brunswick. I'm near the top of the highest mountain."

"Remember I mentioned something about a new development? Well, it hasn't been announced yet, but someone has asked that the whole area from Green Valley to Fundy National Park be rezoned."

"Into what?" Rae asked.

"The province's newest and most exclusive gated community." Louis looked well pleased. "Your land is a stumbling block."

"I'm not following you."

Hunter pursed his lips. Rae didn't know Louis like he did. The old man had dabbled in the markets, skimming off his share, and buying land to sell later for huge profits, especially after he'd laid out rumors, and fake documentation when necessary, of possible increases in land values.

Hunter knew what his friend was leading toward. "Is this legitimate?"

Louis grinned. "Apparently it's all aboveboard, though still in the early stages."

Rae set down her fork. "What do you mean by that?"

The old man's grin softened to a patient smile. "The proposed exit from the highway to this subdivision would run right through your land. Now, this is quite hush-hush. It took a lot for me to get the information. While this is wonderfully interesting, the best part is who owns the land beside you, and who would profit the most from this rezoning."

"Besides one neighbor, there's only government land beside me. . . ." She gasped. "Andy Morrison has been buying the land around me so he can sell it at a huge profit?"

"No. Morrison is only suspected of doctoring the books, that's all."

"Part of Louis's conviction included a faked purchase of public land," Hunter told Rae.

"Ahh, for the good old days," the old man quipped merrily as he reached for a croissant. "For which I have been forgiven," he added hastily.

"Do you think that my father bought the land? He had the money." Rae sat back, eyes wary. Hunter knew she wanted the truth, and again that truth caught in his throat.

All he could do was reach out and touch

her hand, readying himself for anything. Especially considering that half of Benton's life insurance was still missing. He turned to Louis. "Did Benton buy it?"

"No. The alleged owner is Christine Stanton, Constable Halloway's wife and real estate agent extraordinaire."

FIFTEEN

Hunter couldn't believe his ears. He shook his head. The guy whose life he'd saved in prison? His wife had bought the land illegally?

Louis sat down and helped himself to breakfast, then continued. "This Miss Stanton, or Mrs. Halloway, is heavily involved in big real estate deals. *Oui.* Now, it's interesting that she would be privy to information that would profit her, but considering her husband conceivably has inside sources . . ."

Rae leaned forward. "How could a police officer get that information?"

"When I was arrested, they had completed an in-depth investigation into real estate misdealings. Mostly mine, of course." Louis poured himself a coffee. "I pleaded guilty, so much of what the police learned never made it to trial." He shrugged. "But they learned enough to suspect Morrison, though our activities were not related." Hunter glanced at Rae. She was gaping. He set down his mug. "You're telling us that it's possible Mike Halloway's profiting from the knowledge acquired during a previous investigation?"

Louis shrugged again, raising Hunter's ire even more. "How else would she learn about it?"

Hunter blew out a heavy sigh. "But how would Halloway and his wife profit from our deaths? And what about Morrison's disappearance?"

"I don't know, but —"

Rae cut in. "Wait a minute! You're actually thinking that Halloway is trying to kill me over land?"

"My dear," the old man said quietly, "we're only speculating."

Hunter folded his arms. "His wife did visit you, Rae, asking if you planned to sell. And when she found out the land was jointly owned, the attempts on both our lives were accelerated."

"And Halloway was alone with my truck just before the brakes failed," Rae added.

Louis's face lit up. "When was this?"

"Last night, early, before we went to the hotel," she answered. "Wait! Can you find out what kind of vehicle Halloway owns?"

"I may be able to."

Hunter knew that meant yes. He nodded to her.

"Halloway could have been driving a police SUV when you went off the road. It would be risky, but if he is involved in illegal dealings, he may be desperate. I'll see what I can find out." Louis glanced at his food, almost painfully.

Rae read the look, saying, "Eat first, while it's hot."

He smiled gratefully and ate swiftly. When he was done, he excused himself. Rae offered to clear away the dishes while he looked for information on Halloway's car.

Hunter rose with her, announcing that he'd help. Following Rae into the kitchen, he almost ran into her when she stopped to gaze around the room.

"It's like something out of a magazine!"

He mentally cataloged the details. With stainless steel appliances, marble counters and slate floors, the whole room was the epitome of wealth and luxury. Right down to the flat-screen TV beside the refrigerator.

He found its remote control. "Let's watch television while we clean up. I don't know when I'll have another opportunity like this."

"No wonder he thinks this place is too

opulent now." Still shaking her head, Rae began to rinse the dishes. Hunter cruised through the channels.

"Hey, you volunteered to help. Quit surfing and put the leftovers away."

He selected a local morning show, then began to search for storage containers.

". . . and in an incident that might be related to shots fired in downtown Moncton last night, the police are still looking for two people wanted in connection with the disappearance of a local man this week."

Rae froze. Hunter straightened from his task of peering in cupboards. Both stared at the TV. Their driver's license pictures flashed onto the screen.

"Rae-Anne Benton and Hunter Ian Gordon are considered by the police as 'persons of interest.' Both disappeared after being questioned. And after meeting with the police, the mayor is asking why Benton and Gordon were not arrested, considering the evidence against them concerning missing Green Valley man Andrew Morrison —"

Hunter clicked off the TV, then turned to Rae. She'd gone pasty white.

"I wasn't questioned! And they let you go because there wasn't enough evidence."

"Calm down, Rae. Let them say what they want."

Louis hurried into the kitchen. "I just found out that the police have already talked to the taxi driver who dropped you off at the bottom of the hill. It won't take them long to connect you to me."

Hunter scrubbed his hands up and down his face. Louis took the plate Rae was holding. "You two must leave. I reserved a small lodge up north, to take in some duck hunting this week. I'll call them and ask if I can have it a few days earlier. It shouldn't be a problem."

"A cabin on a lake is hardly secure, Louis," Hunter chided.

His friend looked smug. "This will meet your needs for security, believe me."

Rae stepped forward. "We'll stick out like sore thumbs!"

Hunter shook his head thoughtfully. "Not if we look like we're duck hunting. And a lot of wives join their husbands now."

"Exactly." Louis waved at the dishes. "Forget this mess. I've got some clothes and a suitcase you can borrow. Oh, and a pair of camouflage jackets. If you need anything more, get it before you arrive. I think, however, that Rae should do the buying. You're rather recognizable, my friend."

Hunter felt Rae's eyes skim over his scars. "I don't want you going into stores alone."

She touched his arm. "I'll be fine, and I'll blend in better than you."

"I promised your father I'd take care of you."

"And I promised him I'd help you get back on your feet. We'll be able to do both up north, just not the way we originally thought, right?" She quickly dried her hands on the small towel hanging from a nearby hook, and rounded the island that held the sink and dishwasher. "Louis, you've been more than generous. I hate to leave you with all of this."

Louis waved away her concern. "It'll give me something to do. But you both must hurry. The police could show up at any time. Now, I have an old sedan that is still registered in my ex-wife's name. You can use it."

"We can't take your car," Hunter exclaimed.

"My ex-wife's, you mean. Don't worry. I only drive it in the wintertime, hoping it'll rust out. But, like my memories of her, it keeps hanging in there."

After he helped them throw some old clothes into a spare suitcase, he hurried them through the kitchen and into the three-car garage attached to the house, rattling off directions.

Louis leaned in the open window of the old blue Datsun. "Be careful. And watch out for dark green SUVs. I discovered that Halloway owns one. Meanwhile, I'll continue my research here. Ms. Stanton may want your land, but she can't waltz in and take it after killing you."

"Thanks, Louis," Hunter exclaimed.

"Don't mention it. I'll be praying for you." He shook Hunter's hand. "I see I'm out of touch with the local corruptness. In fact, I'm feeling a bit outraged at it all. Perhaps I'll set up my own vigilante group and expose them all." He laughed. "I do have a bit of expertise in this area."

Hunter pulled out of the garage. "That man. One minute he's praying for us, the next he's contemplating a vigilante war."

Rae twisted around to wave goodbye. "It's hard to believe he was a criminal."

"They're — we're not all dirty slobs with shifty eyes, Rae."

"I know." Her words were so soft he barely heard them.

They took a back road for a bit before easing onto the highway at a little-used intersection.

"We should call the police, Hunter," she finally said. "If one of their own is corrupt, they need to know."

He shook his head. This was why she shouldn't be told about the stolen wood. With her strong sense of righteousness, she'd be torn between dismay and her loyalty to her father.

Did that mean he wasn't? Should he have come clean about what he and Benton had done?

"This doesn't feel right," Rae was saying. "Yes, Halloway appears suspicious, but you can't tell me that both our instincts on this man are wrong."

Hunter pursed his lips. While the officer didn't appear to like him, Hunter had been comfortable with him. The cop had been nothing but professional.

"And this only makes us look even more guilty. You didn't get released from prison last week to head back there again. Ten years is enough."

He threw her a dark scowl. She grabbed his arm. "We can't both be wrong about Halloway. Besides, like Louis said, what benefit would it be to the constable if I died? There's something wrong here, Hunter."

She leaned forward to capture his attention. "You don't have any reason at all to trust him, I know. But you don't have any reason not to, either. You've got to start trusting. We can't run away. Dad and I didn't when we had to rebuild our workshop. And you didn't when you burned down the place. And we're not going to run away now."

"Rae —"

"No, Hunter, listen. You don't have any reason to trust anyone. Your mom walked out on you, your father, too, long before you could remember him. And the only decent foster parents you had died. I can understand how you feel, but you have to let it go."

His free hand found hers, and she gripped his, hard. "Just this once, please, Hunter. Trust me, and listen to God."

Ahead was a gas station with a phone booth. And not a car in sight. Hunter felt his foot easing over to the brake pedal.

A lump formed in Rae's throat at the rare sight of a public phone booth.

"Call Halloway. We have only our instincts, and I trust them."

Hunter lifted his head, but she couldn't catch the expression in his eyes. He flicked on the signal light and moved off the road. Face averted, he pulled a business card from his jacket pocket before climbing out of the little car. Rae hopped out as well.

Even from the doorway of the phone

booth she could hear the police officer's harsh tone. "Where are you?"

Hunter drew in a breath and told him. Rae glanced around, finding that the gas station had a small coffee shop attached to it. Hunter must have followed her gaze, for he suggested that they meet in there. "We need to talk. Halloway, I've been honest with you. But today, I need you to bring another officer with you."

"I will, don't worry. We'll be there in about half an hour." He hung up.

Rae and Hunter walked into the empty coffee shop. He ordered extra large coffees for both of them. Within five minutes, two businessmen entered. Hunter watched them closely, leaving Rae to follow his gaze.

"Plainclothes officers," he muttered. "They're here to keep an eye on us."

Rae swung around to gape at him in horror. "How do you know?"

"The one in the long coat investigated Louis, and came back to the jail to question him in another case. Come to think of it, it could be the case against Morrison."

Her heart started to pound a bold rhythm in her throat. The only times she'd felt this uncertain were the day the workshop had burned, the day her father died and today. She clung to the large ironstone coffee mug, using the heat to warm her chilled fingers and steady her nerves. Her silent prayer felt disjointed.

Hunter reached over and covered her hand with his own warm one. For a long while, she looked out the window until Halloway, and the officer who'd been with him when he'd come for Hunter, pulled in.

They walked straight through the café, without so much as glancing at the two other men. Rae found her eyes wandering to the counter, where the young waitress watched with nervous interest.

"Get yourselves a coffee," Hunter said. "This may take a while."

The other officer nodded and left. Halloway slid into the seat opposite Hunter, pinning Rae against the cold window. "Perhaps we should talk at the station," he said.

"Relax. I'm not planning to go anywhere, and I have no intention of jeopardizing the safety of anyone in here. Including those two officers over there."

Halloway smiled. "They were in the neighborhood."

"Next time, pick someone who hasn't been at the pen lately."

Surprisingly, Halloway chuckled, then dropped his smile. "What happened to Ms. Benton's truck?"

"What do you know about it?" she asked.

The other officer returned with two large coffees. He slid in beside Hunter, pinning him in. Halloway continued, "We had a report that a truck was in the ravine near Green Valley. We found spent shotgun shells, and some blood. Naturally, we're concerned."

"Blood?" Rae jerked in alarm. "We didn't cut ourselves."

Hunter leaned forward. "There was a rustling sound near the truck. That's when someone fired at us. I heard some scurrying after that, probably a porcupine or a raccoon hiding in a tree. They're big enough to make a lot of noise."

Hunter stared directly at the cop who'd squeezed in beside him. "Whoever ran us off the road chased us. First he rear-ended us, then returned to see if we'd survived. When he found out we had, he tried to finish the job he'd started with the brakes."

Tension swelled in the quiet café. The only noises were the soft dripping of coffee into a glass pot, and the waitress replenishing the napkin dispensers.

"What are you trying to say, Hunter?" Halloway asked.

"If you've already dragged Rae's truck out

of the ravine, you know that the brakes are shot."

"We've had a mechanic look at them." A light dawned on the constable's face. "You think I tampered with them?"

"Did you?"

"No. When would I have had time? And why?"

The other officer frowned and leaned forward to whisper something in Halloway's ear. Rae strained to hear, but couldn't.

Halloway said, "The station's surveillance video would show that I didn't do anything to that vehicle." He stared calculatingly at Hunter, a frown on his face. Finally, he rubbed his forehead. "This isn't about me. This is about you, Hunter."

"Are we suspects in Morrison's disappearance?"

"You're persons of interest."

"Then why did the TV report a comment from the mayor? Why get him involved, if we're not going to be arrested?"

"Ignore it. It's political, with the mayor standing up for justice."

Rae studied the officer's expression. Halloway wasn't going to show his cards all at once; even she knew that. But she wasn't buying his innocent act.

As if oblivious to her suspicions, the

constable kept talking. "All I know is we wanted to speak to you, but you went missing."

Rae gripped the Formica table. "We didn't do anything to Andy! Have you found the body? What evidence do you have? Besides, you let Hunter go, and now you're suggesting that not being seen for less than twenty-four hours is a crime? Who told the media that we're wanted in Andy's death? Morrison was a nuisance, a guy who kept hitting on me, but it's hardly a reason to kill him!"

Her diatribe over, she watched the other officer glance at Halloway. Beyond them, Rae noticed the two plainclothesmen look up from their coffees. She'd been louder than normal. Had they heard her?

The air around her seemed to thicken. She could feel its weight on her tired shoulders.

"What?" she finally blurted. "What's going on?"

Halloway leaned back in the bench seat, his frown deepening as he looked at Hunter.

"We've found Morrison's clothing, covered in his blood, in a Dumpster in Green Valley. There was an anonymous tip to Crime Stoppers. The person said he saw you dump it there."

Sixteen

Hunter set down his mug, careful not to give away any clues to the turmoil within him. Someone not only wanted Rae dead, but also wanted him back behind bars. Another piece of the jigsaw puzzle had just dropped into place. Too bad he couldn't see the big picture yet.

With Hunter in prison, Rae would be vulnerable. If she died and Hunter was locked up for murder, what would be left?

The land. It didn't have any bird's-eye maple, or any other rare species to be exploited. But it was being considered for development. The government had the right to purchase private land at fair market value, so their deaths would hardly be necessary.

He turned his attention back to the immediate problem. "Who found Morrison's clothing? Who's accusing me?"

Halloway asked, "Is it true?"

Rae slapped down her hand. "Wait! This is for a court of law to decide. One man's word against another isn't enough for an arrest if that's what you're thinking of." She lifted her brows and stared at Halloway. "Who told you that lie? You don't believe them, do you? If that person had any sway, you'd have an arrest warrant."

He smiled blandly. "What did you two do when Andy Morrison stopped by that morning?"

Hunter knew enough to realize the officers were repeating their questions in case they'd slip up on their stories. He drilled Halloway with a hard stare. "I blocked a swing Morrison tried to throw my way. I'd had enough of him. Yes, I was mad. He needed some strong-arm tactics to persuade him to leave. He banged his face against the steering wheel and his nose started to bleed. That was all. I didn't kill him."

"And after that?"

Rae cut in. "I came outside. I remember seeing Andy speed off. He was very much alive." She folded her arms. "I never encouraged the guy. Hunter and I went to the restaurant where he eats breakfast to tell him to leave me alone."

"How did you know where he eats breakfast, if you never wanted anything to do with him?"

They'd been through all this before. "We found a receipt on the floor beside the woodstove in the shop, and because the restaurant was near his work, we assumed it was his," Hunter answered. "We also guessed he was the one who loaded the stove with shavings, because he knew they could cause an explosion. He probably dropped the receipt while searching for matches."

Rae leaned forward. "When we went to the restaurant, we found it *was* Morrison's receipt. He orders the same breakfast every day."

Halloway took out a pad and pen and wrote something down. "Were you mad?"

Rae answered. "He'd broken into my workshop and tried to burn it down! Of course I was mad! But Andy wasn't there, or at his workplace."

Halloway slipped his notebook back into his breast pocket. "Did you notice that the locks of your house had been tampered with?"

"No." Rae reddened. "Not until Hunter saved me from being smothered. With everything that's happened lately, I haven't even thought about it."

216

"And yet you still think I tampered with your brakes?"

She lowered her gaze to her empty coffee mug. "I don't know what to think. Andy is a nuisance, but there's no reason for him to kill me. Can I think the same of you?"

Halloway's face turned stony. The other officer shifted, then spoke. "There's no reason why Mike would kill you."

Hunter cut in impatiently. "Someone tried to run us off the road. Then came back to make sure we were dead. That's why I took Rae into Moncton. You'd touched that truck last, so I wasn't about to go to the police. But it turns out that whoever it was found us. He chased us around a hotel, firing potshots at us. You'd know about that. If you say you didn't tamper with Rae's brakes, then go to the hotel. The girl at the front desk is an eyewitness."

"We plan to." The officer looked at Rae. "By the way, your cousin, Annie Dobson, is looking for you, Ms. Benton. She's worried. When she heard you were missing, she and her husband stopped by and demanded an update."

Rae appeared surprised, as if she hadn't expected they'd be concerned. Contritely, she whispered, "Thanks. I'll call her."

Halloway turned back to Hunter. "Where

are you going now?"

Should he tell them? Hunter wondered. Hadn't Rae asked him to trust? If it was just his life, yeah, he'd tell them, but Benton had asked him to watch out for his daughter.

"We've found a lodge up north," Rae announced.

"Where?"

Hunter drew in his breath and gave the name of the place, along with the directions. And offered up a silent prayer that they were doing the right thing.

They left the officers shortly after, and were halfway up the eastern shore of New Brunswick before Rae spoke. She'd fallen silent when they'd ended their conversation with Halloway. Hunter tightened his grip on the steering wheel, aching to know what she was thinking.

He'd been reviewing all his theories and assumptions in his mind. Was Andy Morrison still alive? Maybe protected by Halloway, so that his wife could somehow acquire all the land proposed for rezoning, to sell for an outrageous profit?

Was that what was behind the attempts on their lives? And the accusations that he'd killed Morrison? With Hunter behind bars, and Rae out of the picture, the land could be seized for unpaid taxes. Or if the authorities learned about Benton's and his illegal activities eleven years ago, the land could be seized because a criminal can't profit from his crimes. Benton had used his own property to store the wood.

Hunter flexed his neck muscles, attempting to loosen them. Which theory was it?

As the sign for their turnoff approached, Rae spoke. "You did the right thing, telling Halloway. It's scary trusting for the first time, but . . . I'm glad you did." He felt her hand come to rest on his arm as she continued. "Your life so far hasn't been conducive to trust, but I knew you had it in you to tell Halloway the truth."

"How's that?" Hunter muttered.

"You were honest after you set fire to the workshop. You didn't try to plead not guilty. That's why I knew you could do it."

A hot lump lodged in his throat. He wasn't honest; he'd been framed. But with a troubled past, and a young, overworked public defender taking his case, he'd seen the writing on the wall and given up.

It had all been lies.

Hunter took the exit and drove on in silence. Rae had honed in on his fears and needs, and he realized right then how much he needed her. He'd earned her trust, her compassion.

Had he also earned her love?

She dropped her hand and he felt its absence keenly.

The next turnoff leaped out at him, and he quickly steered the car up the narrow lane. Remembering Louis's directions, he found the lodge, a small complex of log buildings tucked into the forest. The first one displayed the sign Office.

"I'll register us. You'll stand out too much," Rae told him, pulling on one of Louis's old ball caps and tucking her hair up under it. In the oversize cam jacket, she looked like a dozen other hunters' wives.

She climbed out of the truck, leaving him with his thoughts. *You should tell her the whole truth. She'll forgive you now.*

But he still couldn't dishonor Benton's memory.

Fifteen long minutes ticked by, until she finally came out, dangling two keys from her hand. "Lodge three," she said quietly, chewing her lower lip as she pointed to the third log building.

He hadn't driven five feet when she spoke, her tone tentative. "I found out that the lodge has only one bedroom. I hope you don't mind, but I booked you into a bedroom above the office."

He stopped the car and peered up at the

outside stairs on the side of the main building. It had an excellent view of lodge three and was less than thirty feet away. He nodded his approval.

The cottage was almost as luxurious as Louis's home. No wonder he'd chosen this place, where every creature comfort had been considered. A hot tub sat out back on a wide, spacious deck that overlooked the shallow river beyond. Inside, a state-of-the-art entertainment system awaited. And to Hunter's great relief, there was a burglar alarm.

"I should call Annie." Rae had given the opulence nothing more than a cursory glance before walking to the top of the stairs, where a phone sat on a small table. She made her call short and sweet, giving only the most basic of information. Then, after she rang off, she slowly replaced the receiver.

She wet her lips, then swallowed. "I was standing in the office," she began, as if choosing her words carefully, "waiting for the key, and things just fell into place. Old stuff, new stuff, everything. It all made sense suddenly."

What was she talking about? With a shake of his head, Hunter asked, "Old stuff? About what?"

She took his hand, and he could feel hers shaking. "I figured out exactly what happened ten years ago. Even before the workshop burned. I know the truth, Hunter."

SEVENTEEN

Hunter's heart leaped to his throat. There was no way she could have figured it all out in the few minutes she'd spent at the registration desk. He still hadn't figured out everything.

"Old stuff?" he echoed.

"Yes. Before the old workshop burned down."

He repeated her words in his head. This time, she didn't say, "*you* burned down the workshop." A flush of apprehension raced into his face. "It's all old news, Rae. Your father's dead, so it doesn't matter anymore."

"It matters to me and to us. You know that."

He refused to acknowledge her soft words.

"Hunter?" Rae disconnected her hand, brushing his sleeve so lightly he could barely feel it. "My dad visited you in prison. Enough times for you to lead him to the Lord. But what did he say the last time?"

"Why do you need to know?"

"In the hospital, Dad became very agitated. He was adamant that I forgive you and help you get back on your feet. He was really struggling with something, and it wasn't his death. In fact, for that, he had a lot of peace. How soon before he died did he visit you?"

"He came just before he went to the doctor's office that day." Hunter took for granted that she'd know which doctor's appointment he meant. The one where Benton had collapsed. "He was worried about your safety. He didn't know who was threatening you two."

"They must have only just started." Her voice choked up a bit. "But why not just come out and tell you about the danger? He couldn't say anything too incriminating because he might have been overheard."

"Your father was a good man. Look at what he did for me."

"Yes, let's look at that." She dropped her voice to a whisper. "He brought you home, cleaned you up, then he used you, didn't he?"

"Rae, no one gets used unless they want to be." Hunter didn't believe that adage, yet said it just the same.

She lifted her chin. "I loved Dad. He was

good to me, and yes, to you, warning you not to fight, and taking care of you. It's obvious that you've been protecting him, and his memory."

"Whatever you think he's done, remember, he's been forgiven." Hunter stopped, trying to marshal his thoughts. "And whatever has been happening has nothing to do with him. It's about the land."

Rae's voice sounded faraway, and so quiet. "That's not completely true, is it? I was in the lodge office just now, and had this wave of something come over me. I had insisted that you trust Constable Halloway, so I knew I should trust God. Time to walk the walk, so to speak. Time for faith, too. So even though a part of me figured my bank balance was zero, I paid for the rooms with my Interac card."

Hunter held his breath.

"I knew I had to use my Instant Teller card, just like I knew I had prejudged you and Louis. Your friend was so kind to us, I couldn't allow him to pay for this cottage."

She drew a deep breath. "And my account didn't read 'insufficient funds.' Someone deposited enough to cover the bill. You're the only one who would have put money into my account. Did my father give you his life insurance money?"

Here goes. "Half of it."

She stiffened. Hunter forced his arms to stay at his sides, and not pull her into an unwelcomed embrace. At that moment, he hated himself. He shouldn't have had that money. He shouldn't be forced into telling her this. And above all, he hated the corner Benton had backed him into.

"Why?" she asked. "Unless he owed you for something. And where did the other half go?"

The coffee he'd drunk at the café churned sourly in his stomach. "I don't know."

"But you have some ideas, right?"

He did, but he wasn't going to mention them. She'd do the trusting thing and tell the police. He didn't want to risk putting her in any more danger. "Rae, it was for your own safety that we — I kept anything from you."

She lit up. " 'Anything for my safety' really meant something illegal, didn't it? And it's been staring at us all along. I know that crate with the boxing gloves in it was made of bird's-eye maple. I should have asked where Dad got it, but I trusted him.

"Before you both were saved, you and Dad were involved with Cutter and his illegal wood harvest. Cutter went to jail for you two. I'm guessing the minimum-security jail in Moncton, not the federal penitentiary. Dad let him take the fall. So if he was capable of doing that to Cutter, he was capable of doing that to you."

This had to be a bad dream. A band of steel tightened around Rae's chest, and as much as she tried to stop it, the painful truth kept squeezing her.

Lord, I need some strength right now. You're giving me these words, so I need to be able to handle them.

"Rae, let it go."

She grabbed Hunter's arms. "My father framed you, didn't he?" *Oh, Lord, why did Dad do that? What scared him enough to burn down our source of livelihood and frame Hunter?*

A number of frightening answers eddied in her mind.

He pulled back from her. "Rae, it's going to hurt. I told you to let it go. I'm not proud of my past, but I've learned from it."

"When you said that before, I assumed you were talking about the fire. But there's more you're not proud of, isn't there?"

"A bit more," he answered cautiously.

He was still holding back. Suddenly, she needed air. Right now. Too many truths, too quickly . . . Plowing past him and down the stairs, she barely made it to the back deck before her lungs started screaming. Fortunately, a draft of cold air stemmed her panic. She heard Hunter slip outside, too, and she turned to face him. "You didn't want me to know because it's not Christian to speak ill of the dead, or to accuse them. But this isn't an accusation, Hunter. Even the Bible reported the facts, both good and bad, and we should, too. My life has been threatened and my father kept things from me. I loved Dad, and that won't ever change. I'm so grateful that someday my family will be reunited. But in the meantime, I'd like the truth, so that the reunion isn't premature!"

A breeze picked up and, feeling its hint of winter, she shivered.

"Let's go inside, Rae. This isn't a conversation for the outdoors."

She nodded and allowed Hunter to lead her back into the fashionable living room. There, with folded arms and a grim expression, he finally answered. "He gave me the money because I went to prison for him, and because he wanted me to keep you safe. I think he had been trying to tell you, but couldn't."

She shut her eyes. "So you had been stealing trees?"

"Yes. I helped the loggers, a couple of guys from up north who came down looking for work. Cutter used his portable sawmill after."

"So Dad did the rest, like paying the loggers and finding a market. Look, while illegal loggers have taken to carrying shotguns, this isn't enough to kill *me*. Dad could have used half of his insurance money to pay the loggers, but they'd have charged just a few hundred bucks. Getting involved with Andy would have taken more money. Andy sounded paranoid when he was talking to you at the end of the driveway that morning. Saying things like matching lumber to tree stumps, and you and Dad going against him. At first, I thought it was just sour grapes. But the more I think of it, the more it sounds like a natural progression from stealing trees to stealing land. That would take more money."

With a small sense of satisfaction, Rae watched Hunter unfold his arms. Good. She had his attention. As long as he wasn't directly accusing her father, he'd be more forthcoming, she knew. Despite the horror of all that was happening, a soft, mushy swell of emotion rolled through her.

"Go on," he prompted.

She dropped into an armchair, feeling the

weight of her assumptions. Getting used to all the ideas swirling through her seemed to be taking time. Usually, if she felt she was on the right track, her ideas and words flowed easily. This time, each one seemed to sting her. "Andy is being investigated for the illegal sale of government land. I think after you went to prison, Dad changed strategies. Why steal wood, which was becoming a bit too suspicious, when, with a guy who can do some creative bookkeeping, you could own the land the wood is on?"

"The police must have been watching, so that would make him even more desperate to keep you out of it."

She perked up. "That's it, isn't it? Dad figured as long as I knew nothing, I'd be safe from prosecution. He must have felt that the police would believe me if they ever questioned me." She touched her lip, then spoke again. "So he and Andy must have been heavily involved in this scheme. Maybe even Halloway and his wife. Maybe they promised to keep me out of it, if Dad put up the money. After the fire, he must have considered it less risky than having rare wood in his workshop. There was a lot of lumber in the shop before it burned."

Hunter bowed his head.

"With Cutter charged and Dad feeling the

heat, that would be a reason to burn down the shop, and frame you, she mused. "He destroyed any evidence, and since you already had a bad rep, no one would believe you if you did squeal. Is that how it happened, Hunter?"

"Your father sent you to your cousin's house that day." Hunter wiped his face with his hand. "And then he sent me to the garage with the truck. I figured out something was up, so I returned. By that time, he'd already set fire to the place. A week before, he'd told me he had cancer, and when I realized I'd been set up —"

"You knew Dad framed you because he didn't want to die in prison. That's why you didn't fight it."

"How could I ruin what was left of your father's life? He'd saved mine by dragging me off the streets, and mentoring me. He'd given me a purpose, albeit an illegal one, but I knew the risks we were taking, just like Cutter knew them."

"Why didn't Cutter implicate you and my dad?"

"Maybe he tried, and there wasn't enough evidence. I don't know. Maybe your father did promise him money if he stayed quiet."

She shut her eyes. The decade-old memories of returning that evening, after having heard that the workshop was on fire, washed over her.

The intense heat, the cracking of heavy beams being destroyed, the snap and sizzle, a thousand times louder than anything she'd ever heard, the brilliant glare of flames all assaulted her still.

And Dad watching with tears running down his face. She'd hugged him, told them they'd rebuild.

They had. But the new workshop was much smaller, the equipment list shorter, their business's growth potential gone.

That night, Annie and Kirk had taken her to their home. Annie had practiced her mothering skills; Kirk had spent time comforting Benton and later helping to rebuild the shop. The whole awful time in Rae's life still felt so fresh, so painful. Yes, she'd now guessed her father's sins, and yes, she still loved him . . . but she needed time for it all to make sense.

She lifted her head and blinked at Hunter. To the west, the sunset was in full swing, and with the ever-narrowing slit of orange sky, the world had begun to sink into night. She paused. With a deep breath, she said, "Hunter, I need to be alone." She glanced around. "There's got to be a Bible here somewhere. I wish I'd brought mine."

She wanted to pray. She *needed* to pray.

But Hunter was shaking his head. "I'm not leaving. In case you don't remember, someone wants you dead, and we still don't know why."

"We both know this place is safe. No one followed us. So the least thing you can do is give me some breathing space. I need to pray." She tried to reason with him, and plucked at her borrowed shirt. "Not to mention clean up."

His jaw tightened and she knew her logic, not to mention her modesty, was secure. "All right. I have some questions of my own that need answers." He stood. "I'll set the burglar alarm, and you can lock the doors. I'll call to let you know when I'll be back."

He hesitated for a minute, and she held her breath. Would he kiss her goodbye? Did she want him to?

She swallowed. Yes, she wanted him to. But through a haze of tears, she watched him turn away. After setting the alarm, by stabbing the buttons a bit too forcefully, he left her alone.

Even as he shoved Louis's little car into gear, Hunter had no idea where to go first. Morrison's home? Or the police station to ask to see the surveillance tapes from both the hotel and the station? Or should he go back to the workshop to make sure Benton hadn't stashed the leftover insurance money somewhere?

He'd go to the police first. It was the right thing to do.

Shaking his head, he concentrated on his driving, finding a phone booth when he reached the highway. Had Halloway already viewed the security tapes from the hotel? One way to find out.

"Constable Halloway," the voice on the other end announced seconds after Hunter had dialed the number.

"It's Hunter Gordon. Did you get to look at the tapes yet?"

"I have a copy of each right in front of me. I've viewed the hotel's, but there were several people in the lobby at that time, and I still haven't been able to ID them all."

"Did they have any videos of the back of the building? Have you found Andy Morrison yet?"

"No, but I need you two to come down here and view these tapes for yourselves."

Hunter thought of Rae. She needed to be alone before she could completely accept any of the painful truths about her father, even those she'd guessed. "Rae's in no shape to drive back down there. I'll come, though."

"Are you sure you could recognize every-one Ms. Benton's dealt with recently?"

Probably not, but Hunter wasn't going to turn down an opportunity to view the tapes and see the man who was trying to kill them. "I'm sure I can," he stated.

"I'll be here all evening."

Hunter rang off, and a moment later, called the lodge. There was no answer. Alarm hit him, but he quelled it immediately. Rae was probably in the shower or praying. There was no need to interrupt her.

The answering machine kicked in.

"Rae, it's me. I'm going down to see Halloway about a few things. I'll be back as soon as I can."

At the Green Valley police station, Halloway escorted him into a back room that housed a table, some chairs and a video system. The officer slid the tape into the VCR and they waited, both men standing with arms crossed.

The grainy video showed an older couple, and then a family who talked briefly with the woman behind the desk.

Finally, a man of medium build approached. The receptionist talked with him briefly and the man nodded.

Hunter peered hard at the tape, while Halloway reached forward to pause it.

The security camera must have been quite high, and looking down on the people made it difficult to recognize them. The man kept his head down, and a thick coat zipped up. An ordinary man. Older than him, maybe, with a mess of dark hair. Average build, yet familiar.

Where had he seen him before?

The answer danced just outside of his reach.

"Can I get a still picture of this guy?"

Halloway hesitated.

Hunter peered into the officer's eyes. "The hotel wants this incident solved as quickly and quietly as possible, right? Without anyone spreading bad publicity. So, naturally, that would mean allowing the police to have some stills."

Halloway smiled and reached into his shirt pocket. He pulled out a folded photograph.

Hunter took it. "Where are you going with the picture? Just so we don't overlap?"

He shrugged. "I figured I would start in Green Valley. The guy's hair looks fake, but someone may recognize his build."

His mouth tight, Hunter stared again at the picture. "He seems familiar, but it's not a great snapshot. Did you compare it with the video from the compound?"

Halloway looked impressed. "We have only a very short clip of someone near Ms. Benton's truck. Nothing that even comes close to this in quality. Are you headed back up north?"

"Eventually. I have a couple of things to do first."

The constable nodded. "If you find out anything, I want to be the first to know. Not a lawyer, not Ms. Hunter. Me. Understand?"

Hunter nodded. "I will. But first, I'd like to talk to Andy Morrison." He wasn't prepared to say anything more yet.

"Really?" Halloway said. "Well, you'll be interested to know that this guy isn't Andy Morrison."

"How do you know for sure?"

"He showed up this afternoon to take back possession of his car, saying he'd gone on a binge."

"Did you arrest him?"

Halloway's eyes narrowed. "What for?"

It was Hunter's turn to shrug. "Public mischief?"

"No. He was allowed to take his car and go home. He didn't make a complaint against you, either."

"Did he say where'd gone? Did you ask?"

This time the officer offered nothing.

Hunter knew that they'd asked, but hadn't pressed the issue.

"Did he look like he'd been out drinking?" Hunter had seen plenty of that early in his life. He knew the evidence of days wasted on booze. Dirty, even ripped clothes, the stink of liquor and cigarettes. Bleary eyes, disorientation, lashing out at people. He'd seen all that when he'd been too little to defend himself.

Halloway cut into his memories. "If you're asking how we know it wasn't him, he's limping badly. His ankle is the size of his thigh, and he's nursing some shoulder problems, too. He said he doesn't remember how he got hurt."

"Do you believe him?"

Halloway's shrug told Hunter he didn't. But with shots fired in Moncton, the police would be busy. Even Green Valley's police, if there was a suspicion of their residents being involved. Hunter knew he was lucky to have learned all he had. The cops were keeping closemouthed, that's all.

"The point is, the guy in the video is walking just fine. So unless Morrison hurt himself after that, he couldn't have fired at you at the hotel. But his ankle looked like it had been hurt days ago."

■ ■ ■ ■

Rae dragged herself off the bed, feeling as if she'd been hit by a freight train several times over. Her swollen eyes throbbed in rhythm with the booming pulse behind them. Her prayers had been difficult and jumbled, until she'd finally dropped off to sleep.

The clock by the bed showed it was nearly eight in the evening. As hard as it was for her to believe, she'd actually fallen asleep for several hours. She'd prayed for a while after Hunter had left, until she felt the need to talk to someone. Annie was the only person who came to mind, but when she'd tried her cousin's number, there was no one home. Reluctant to leave a message, she'd simply hung up and collapsed onto the bed.

Beside the clock, the phone flashed, indicating a message was waiting. She leaned over, hit the button and listened to Hunter's voice.

A lump lodged in her throat. He had gone to prison for a crime her dad had committed. And now was doing everything he could for her. But Dad had turned his life around . . .

Surprisingly, she felt a jolt of fury. At Dad?

At herself for guessing the truth, or at Hunter for reluctantly confirming her suspicions?

Lord, help me to forgive everyone. And not to shoot the messenger.

Rae rolled off the bed and trudged to the bathroom. There, she splashed water on her face before pressing a wet facecloth against her swollen, tired eyes.

Why would someone want her share of Benton land? Then she remembered what Louis had said about the new development of a fancy gated community. But killing her wouldn't guarantee owning the land. She hadn't willed it to anyone, so should she die, her cousins, now scattered around New Brunswick and British Columbia, would just have to split her share of the estate.

She squinted against a growing headache. What she really needed was something to eat and a hot cup of tea. Maybe then she'd be able to think better.

She eased herself down the stairs, hating that she probably wouldn't find any painkillers in the lodge.

In the kitchen, however, she found tea, coffee, sugar, even a small carton of milk and another of cream. There were also some crackers and small packs of jam, and a tin of local salmon.

As swiftly as she could, she made herself hot tea, and with a packet of crackers, sat down at the café table that looked onto the back lawn, straight down to the wide, shallow river that was world famous for salmon fishing. Up north here, the leaves had already relented to the cold winds of late fall, and all that remained were stark gray trees, dark firs and pine and the cold, swift course of the river.

She was taking her third sip when she heard a car roll past the lodge. It reached the end of the drive and turned around. Standing, she peered out the front window as it pulled up to her cottage.

A light-colored Saturn, much like a thousand others on the road.

But who was driving it surprised her.

EIGHTEEN

Back to square one, Hunter thought, staring at Halloway after he'd told him the news. Morrison couldn't have walked into that hotel? Nor driven them off the road, then slid down the ravine after them? So who did?

"How do you know Morrison hurt himself before yesterday?"

Halloway reached for a file sitting on his desk, then thought better of it and pulled his hand back. "His ankle is purple and yellow, and that tells me it couldn't have been injured last night. It has to have been done shortly after he met you at Benton's Woodworking."

Hunter's mind whirring, he asked, "Did you know your wife stopped by to see Rae? She asked her if she was willing to sell her property. And was surprised to learn that I was a half owner, as well."

There was no look of shock on Halloway's

face. Everyone else was shocked, surprised, disgusted even, that Hunter owned part of Benton Woodworking. But not Halloway. He'd already known.

"And you knew it, didn't you? Did your wife tell you?"

"My wife runs the busiest real estate agency in the city. I don't keep track of her business dealings."

"But she told you. Right?"

Halloway didn't answer.

"Look, she showed up asking Rae to sell. Now, some may say that coming right after a funeral isn't in good taste. I don't want you to think I'm judging her, but something sounds wrong." Hunter waited, but when the officer didn't speak, he went on. "Halloway. Mike. Even a ruthless real estate agent is going to give a person some time to mourn."

"Christine didn't get to be the best by sitting and waiting for things to come to her."

"Yes, she's the best agent in the area, but she doesn't have a reputation for being cruel. She came with a purpose, and she left pretty quickly after she discovered that I was co-owner. That wasn't expected."

"My wife doesn't tell me every detail of her day."

"But she told you about me, didn't she?

243

Rae's lawyer, LeBlanc, wouldn't have told anyone, and no one else knew."

"So what if she told me?"

Hunter leaned back in his seat. "Because the only reason she'd tell you would be if you needed to know. And the only reason you'd need to know would be if there was some investigation going on."

Halloway fiddled with various items on his desk. Finally, he stood and said, "We need to talk privately."

He led the way into an interrogation room. Hunter glanced up at the video monitoring system. "Is this room private?"

"The equipment's not on. Believe me, neither of us wants it on right now." He shut the door. "Tell me what you know."

Hunter sat in the nearest chair. "Your wife asked Rae to sell. Normally, the land wouldn't be worth much, unless it was going to be rezoned as part of some elite facility. And you would conceivably have inside information on that."

"How would I get that kind of information?"

"When Louis Carriere was arrested, the police completed an in-depth investigation into real estate fraud. I'm thinking a lot more than what Louis was found guilty on was exposed."

"And you think I'm profiting from knowledge gained during that investigation?"

"No. It's far too difficult to buy public land, and yet, according to Louis's sources, your wife has bought public land that wasn't officially for sale. Morrison cooked the books to make it possible, but Rae and I don't think you're involved in anything illegal."

Halloway blew out a heavy sigh. "A gut feeling? All right. Listen. I don't want to say this, but I have to. Christine *is* involved. We needed an officer who knows real estate inside and out. Someone who could gain Morrison's confidence. Christine has always loved dabbling in buying and selling land, and is determined enough to convince anyone of anything." He smiled wryly. "She convinced me I couldn't live without her."

Hunter felt a chill trickle down his neck. He glanced up at the video camera. He hadn't wanted it on, and now was regretting that it wasn't.

"Carriere is right. We've been investigating Morrison. Christine and a man from the provincial government helped with figuring it all out. They became the front line in all of this. I didn't want her involved, but Christine is tough. She was once an auxiliary police officer."

"Where did Robert Benton fit into all this?"

"He wanted to get involved, and he was to a certain extent, but he didn't have enough money to do everything Morrison had planned. I think the cancer made him want to give his daughter a bit more money, so he took the risks."

Hunter exhaled. Benton had tried to make a bit of money with the illegal harvest of government trees, some of which were rare and expensive, but when Cutter Stevenson was arrested, he'd changed tactics. "Did your wife contact them first or vice versa?"

Halloway looked uncomfortable. "This is an ongoing investigation."

"Rae's life is in danger, Mike!"

"The investigators made initial contact. We believe that Morrison then realized he was going to need more money than what they already had."

"Just Morrison?"

"We believe so. But about two months ago, Benton backed out of the dealings and began to attend church. Shortly after, we realized that he wouldn't survive much longer, so we decided to cease investigating him for the purpose of attaining a conviction."

"But after Christine left, the attempts on

Rae's life started. Who is trying to kill us? Morrison wouldn't profit from our deaths."

"Who would? Who are your relatives?"

"I have no one. My mother left years ago, and is probably dead by now. I have no father, and only one brother somewhere. I'm a write-off relativewise."

"Rae?"

They stared at each other. "Let's see that tape again," Hunter suggested.

Rae walked to the door, wondering how Kirk had found where she was staying. Through Annie, most likely, she decided. Annie had already gone to the police about Rae's safety. She had a bulldog streak in her a mile wide. But would Halloway tell her where to find them?

Rae doubted that. Kirk had probably used caller ID and the Internet to locate the lodge's address.

Annie had probably sent Kirk up here to talk her into coming back to their place.

It wouldn't work. She could get rid of Kirk easily enough. He wasn't the kind to want to deal with weepy women, so it wouldn't take much convincing to get him to head back home.

Rae opened the door for him, and with an almost surprised look on his face, he stepped over the threshold.

"I'm not going home with you, Kirk. I'm fine. I just want to be alone."

Kirk looked around. "Whoa! How can you afford this?"

Rae was about to blurt out that she had the money, but the words caught in the back of her throat. Why was that question the first thing out of his mouth? "I hate to turn you around so soon after you've come all this way, but frankly, I *need* to be alone." She stood by the open door.

He didn't move. "I know you want to be by yourself, Rae, but you shouldn't be."

Feeling a draft, she shut the door. Just as she did so, she spied the Saturn again. "Whose car is that, anyway?"

"A friend's. I borrowed it."

"It's a long way to drive with a borrowed car. What happened to your truck?"

"I hit a deer last night and damaged the front end."

The hairs on her neck tingled and she walked to the window to peer out. "It looks like Andy Morrison's car."

"It is."

She turned. Kirk was busy perusing the living room, lifting his eyebrows at the sight of the entertainment center.

"You saw Andy Morrison? Isn't he still

missing? I thought the police had his vehicle?"

Kirk shrugged. "He showed up yesterday and took it back. I borrowed it. No big deal."

Something didn't sound right, but she couldn't think what. There was too much on her mind to deal with Kirk and with Annie, who constantly insisted on mothering her.

Like those days after the fire.

Why had Dad insisted she visit Annie that day, when he hadn't ever done so before? Annie and Kirk were a young couple, childless, busy. Rae's father hadn't bothered with them too much after they'd settled into their life together.

Other small clues trickled in. Her father's odd behavior; the stoic stubbornness Hunter had displayed when he'd said, only once, "I didn't burn down the workshop." Everyone simply thought he'd been lying.

Lord, I understand. I will accept the truth.

"You look awful, Rae. You should come home with me. Go upstairs and pack."

She blinked at Kirk. He was never one to press a person. He simply didn't care enough. Annie was the one who cared. But if Hunter had run into Kirk after he'd called her . . .

"Why are you here, Kirk?"

"Annie sent me. She's worried sick. And I'm sick of listening to her howl at me for not doing more for you."

While his answer was logical, even expected to a certain degree, something didn't feel right about it. Annie wouldn't just send Kirk. She'd come, too, not trusting him to deliver the compassion she knew would be needed to convince Rae to come home with her.

Rae bit her lip. Suddenly, she wished Hunter was here. With his insight, he'd know what to do.

He had more than intuition. He cared for her.

"I'm not leaving. I'm waiting for Hunter to come back."

Kirk's face lit up as he exclaimed, "I forgot! I ran into Hunter at a gas station on the road up here. I spotted him getting gas, and I told him what Annie wanted to do. He thought it was a good idea, too. He said he'd meet you at our place."

"He said that?" Rae frowned. That didn't make sense. He'd left a message on the machine saying that he was going to see Halloway and that he'd be back as soon as he could.

Wouldn't he have called again?

But if Hunter had met Kirk after the call . . . perhaps he hadn't had a chance to call back. At times like this, she wished for the intrusion of a cell phone.

"Yeah, that's what he said."

She took a step toward the phone. "Maybe he's already at your place now. I should call."

She picked up the phone and studied the long distance instructions on the base.

Abruptly, Kirk swung his arm around her and slammed it up against her throat. She gasped, grabbed at his forearm, only to have him press tighter.

If she didn't do something in the next few seconds, Kirk would strangle her to death.

Nineteen

His hand over the phone, Halloway told Hunter, "Rae's not at the cabin."

Standing in Halloway's cubicle, Hunter pushed back the alarm growing in him. "Did the manager see how she left? Did she call a taxi? She wouldn't have walked away!"

Halloway's expression had turned grim. "A guest saw a light colored car drive off. He didn't see who was at the wheel."

Hunter's heart lodged in his windpipe. He spun around, but was caught by the officer before he could leave.

"Hunter! It can't be Morrison!"

"It's not! It's Kirk Dobson! I bet he has Morrison's car. He owns a truck like the one that pursued us — I remember the headlight style. He must have damaged it when he hit us! That's why he's not driving it."

"How could he have found her? How could he get Morrison's car?"

"Who cares about that! We need to find out where he took her."

The workshop. The answer dropped into his head, clear and obvious. "Benton Woodworking. He wants me there so he can frame me. He's planning on burning down the workshop."

"Why?" Halloway grabbed the videotape from the machine before Hunter pushed past him. "Wait! Why would Kirk do that?"

"There's no time to explain. If you're not coming with me, you'd better follow quickly."

Hunter plowed down the hall, startling a young clerk at the front entrance. Everyone looked back at Halloway, who said something Hunter didn't catch. Louis's old beat-up car started on the first crank, thankfully, allowing Hunter to rip away from the curb.

Oh, Father, keep her safe. Keep her safe!

"The only thing that's wrong is that you won't give up."

Kirk tightened his stranglehold on Rae, and she fought back the panic that threatened to overwhelm her. He gripped harder and harder as she struggled wildly to free herself. She scratched and clawed at his arms, but her short nails had little effect.

253

She kicked him savagely in the shins and twisted fiercely to escape.

Nothing did any good. Kirk might not be a tall man, but he was all muscle, stocky and strong. And he kept tightening his grasp on her.

Spots appeared before her eyes, and her head felt as if it might explode at any moment. Her neck muscles cramped, and she knew she had only seconds left.

All she could do now was go limp. An instant later, blackness wove through her vision.

Then there was the bliss of nothingness.

Rae came to in total darkness. She tried to stretch out, but her feet and head bumped hard against walls.

Or something hard. She tried to lift her head from the gritty, uneven carpet, only to crack it on the metal ceiling of whatever she was trapped in.

She was being rolled and knocked about, and whatever was sharing the small space bumped against her.

What was going on? She shook off the dredges of unconsciousness and drew a deep breath. Her throat felt as if it were on fire.

Yes, she remembered. Kirk! He'd tried to

strangle her, and when she'd fallen unconscious, he must have stuffed her into the
trunk of Andy's car. She could hear the
deep bass of some hard rock music thrumming through the vehicle.

But why on earth would Kirk do this? The
look on his face told her he wasn't dragging
her back to his and Annie's house because
his wife was worried about her.

He'd had murder in his eyes.

The car hit another brutal bump and
knocked her about. Then it turned, and
something long and heavy and cold rolled
against her.

She grabbed it, and then, belatedly, let
out a scream. She'd grabbed an arm. The
cold, slightly clammy, hair-roughened arm
of a man.

"Ugh!" she cried, brushing the horrid
thing away.

But it rolled back again.

She was stuffed in the trunk of a car with
a body.

Was it Hunter? No. There was no way
Kirk could overpower him. Except if he had
a gun, as he'd had when he'd run them
down, following them and finally chased
them from the hotel last night.

As much as she could, she squirmed away,
pressing against the back of the car even

though the lock mechanism dug into her right hip. With her knees, she shoved the body away. Turning, she scraped her hand against something luminescent.

A glow-in-the-dark trunk release handle.

The car turned, slowed and turned again. She felt it bump over some potholes.

Now or never.

She yanked on the handle and the trunk flew open. In the next second, she sprang free, tumbling over the rear bumper head-first.

Gravel met her with a hard scraping thud. Her arms, thankfully wrapped in long sleeves, plowed like a snow shovel into the dirt and stones, and her legs splayed out painfully.

Dazed, she took a moment to absorb her situation. She'd held her head high to prevent road rash on her face, but paid the price now of Kirk's stranglehold. Her whole neck burned like fire.

Behind her, the car screeched to a stop, and she heard a door open. Glancing around, she saw they'd reached her house.

Why go back where people would expect her to be?

Swearing, Kirk raced up to her. Aching, she twisted around, then struggled to her feet.

But not soon enough. He grabbed her, pinning her arm back and clamping his forearm in front of her throat again. "You just won't give up, will you?"

She gasped, kicked and fought against him.

He dragged her into her workshop, clenching even harder as he unlocked its main door.

He had a key? With her vision swimming, Rae guessed that he'd had one all these years. *Of course.* He'd installed the locks when they were building the workshop.

Did that mean he'd also tried to set fire to the place the other day? She tried again to fight him off, but ended up stumbling over the threshold. "Kirk," she rasped. "What are you doing? Let me go! Are you insane?"

He threw her into the chair by her desk, and before she could lunge away, pulled her arms back and locked her left wrist to the back of the chair with an electrical tie-down. She battled to free herself, at the same time fighting the panic that swamped her. Lashing out at him with her feet, she managed to trip him, and he stumbled and fell.

He leaped up. When he turned, she jerked back. His face had twisted into a terrifying mask. He cursed her long and loudly, and with a sweep of his hand slapped her face.

"You're a fool, woman! Just like all of them. Cutter, Morrison, your father. You're sitting on a gold mine and you have no idea what to do! And Morrison with his stupid idea of marrying you instead of getting rid of you! I had to threaten him with going to the police if he didn't start doing something. But he bungled that fire he started."

"And you did the rest, even deciding that Andy had to die?"

"Why not? You're all small-time! Your father was ready to take advantage of all our plans, then he backed out of his end of the deal! He found God!"

From his pocket, Kirk pulled out a roll of duct tape, and after pinning her head between his solid chest and his arm, he managed to slap a strip across her mouth.

She tried to reach up to peel away the tape, but he twisted her arm back. Then he shoved a pen into her hand and wheeled her toward her desk. On it was a long document. "Sign it. In your normal handwriting. If you don't, I'll kill Hunter. If you do, he merely goes to prison again for arson."

On the desk was one of those generic packaged wills, already made out with her name. She wanted to refuse, but when she hesitated, he grabbed her arm roughly. "Sign it or Hunter dies!"

Hand shaking, she did so. She was willing her estate to Kirk.

After Kirk stuffed the will into his pocket, he dug out another electrical tie-down and secured her right hand to the back of the chair. Then he grabbed her swinging feet and, with strength she had no idea he possessed, strapped them to the center pole of the swivel chair.

Panic roared through her. She couldn't pull in a deep enough breath through her nostrils. Tears sprang into her eyes, and her throat burned from Kirk's attempts to subdue her.

Now her legs ached from the unnatural position.

Shoving her back against a small filing cabinet, Kirk stood, then left her. He returned a moment later with the body she'd felt beside her, now slumped over his shoulder. He dumped it on the damp floor in front of the woodstove.

Rae strained to see who it was. *Please let it not be Hunter. Please, Lord?*

The man unrolled onto his back.

Andy Morrison. Rae sucked in her breath.

Sickened and yet unable to look away, she watched as Kirk took a small jerrican of gasoline she'd stored out back, and splashed it onto some wood scraps. After throwing the pieces into the firebox, he trickled some of the gas onto Andy's hands.

Lord, help me!

Her eyes widened as Kirk carefully took a soft rag and wiped down every place he'd touched, from the duct tape on her mouth to the woodstove door. Afterward, he gingerly pulled the tin of matches from its place high above the stove. She and Hunter had used those matches this week, she recalled, watching Kirk delicately retrieve a few, without leaving any fingerprints in the process.

Please, no! She pleaded with her eyes, but he didn't notice. He struck one match and let it burn out. Then he struck another and flung it into the stove.

Whomp! The small fireball exploded inside and she heard the flue rattle in protest. Over the smell of the workshop, damp from the air and Hunter's frequent mopping, the odor of gasoline swirled around her.

She stared helplessly up at Kirk.

He smiled at her. "Oh, yes, I've got it all figured out, thanks to all those forensic shows on TV." He chuckled, then sighed as he lit another match and dropped it onto Andy's limp hand.

Rae shut her eyes, expecting another explosion of flames.

When she opened them a second later, Kirk was gone. And the match he'd dropped had gone out on its journey to the cold floor.

With the stove door still open and the scraps inside, burning fiercely, she watched as the sparks flew about.

Please, Lord! Please put that fire out!

She lurched forward, her knees and shoulder bearing her weight as she fell onto the damp floor. With awkward movements, she clambered toward Andy, watching with horror the sparks that danced too close to the front of the firebox and the evaporating gasoline.

The spilled fuel leading to his body still hadn't caught fire! The cement floor was too damp from the recent rains . . . and Hunter's persistent need to keep things clean.

Suddenly, beside her, Andy moaned and shifted.

She gasped. He was alive!

She tried to shut the stove door, but being unable to latch it, she could only watch helplessly as it swung back open. Desperately, she clamped her knees around Andy's head and started to drag him away from the fire. Still bound to the chair, she inched toward the door, and away from the heat of the fire.

Even if she did reach the door, she wouldn't be able to open it, not pulling Andy.

Halfway there, she collapsed to the concrete.

All the while praying that Kirk wasn't going after Hunter next.

Hunter raced down the wide street, cutting through the new subdivision, as Rae often did, to save time. He drove through a stop sign, thankful that the intersection was empty.

The traffic remained light, but he was still ten minutes away from Rae's house.

And that was assuming Kirk had taken her there.

He had to have done so. It was the only logical place. Kirk wanted Rae's land, and the only thing in his way was the fact that Hunter owned half. Had Rae willed her share to Annie?

What about *his* share? Since Hunter had supposedly burned the workshop down before, he'd probably be charged with doing so again. And off to prison, likely losing the land on his way.

No, this time would be different. He wasn't going to take the rap for it again.

Hunter spun off toward the west. Driving

far too recklessly, he sped past another series of quiet homes and finally up the rolling hill he and Rae owned.

Through the car's vents, he caught a whiff of smoke.

Father, let it be some landowner burning brush.

His heart pounded in his throat. His fingers ached from clutching the steering wheel. And as he closed in on Rae's home, he knew with increasing certainty and dread that the smoke was indeed coming from her workshop.

With his foot hard on the gas pedal, he urged the little rattletrap of a car up the hill. He strained to peer out the windshield, upward, to search the nearly leafless forest ahead for the truth.

Rae's house loomed before him, and he cranked the wheel hard to steer over the culvert and into the driveway.

With eyes shut, Hunter dropped his head onto the steering wheel. Like ten years ago, when he'd guessed the truth about what Benton had planned, he was too late.

The workshop was engulfed in flames.

TWENTY

Hunter snapped his head up. The hairs on his neck stood erect, and his breath jammed in his throat. Without understanding how, he knew that Rae was in the burning building.

Far in the distance, he could hear sirens. Someone had alerted the fire department, perhaps a neighbor. He glanced down the road. A small car was parked in a driveway ahead of him. Thankfully, someone was around.

He threw open the car door, alit from the vehicle and galloped toward the workshop.

Please, Lord God . . .

The entire back of the building was burning. From the woodstove. Thick smoke was blasting up and around the chimney. When he reached the door, he gingerly tapped the knob, testing it for heat. It wasn't scorching, so he pushed it open.

Smoke rolled out, desperate to escape.

Blinking, he bent down to peer through the rising blanket of white.

Yes! His heart leaped in his chest, and with the resulting gasp took in a lungful of dense smoke. He coughed it out and dropped to the floor.

Rae! She lay ahead of him, wrapped around the desk chair. Her eyelids fluttered open at the draft of fresh air that had rolled in along the floor. Her frightened eyes met his.

Then, from behind, something hit him. Stumbling, Hunter rolled over and kicked hard at whoever was attacking him. His foot struck something soft — a leg? Rae let out loud, urgent moans — she couldn't speak. Was that duct tape covering her mouth? Hunter scrambled toward her, only vaguely aware of a figure limping out and slamming the door behind him.

Reaching Rae, Hunter tried to free her from the chair, but she didn't budge. Dobson had done a nasty job tying her up. Hunter scanned her face, then tore off the wide strip of tape.

Rae pulled in a deep breath, followed by a fit of weak coughing. She tried to say something, but her coughs choked off the words.

Still kneeling, he dragged her along the

floor. He wanted to haul her up, chair and all, but that would mean she'd have her head in the smoke. When he reached the door, he scooped her up and pulled her outside.

The sirens were closer now. Hunter carried Rae to the end of the driveway and off to his left. He placed her gently, chair and all, on a bed of leaves.

She'd fallen unconscious.

Doing a quick scan, he found the reason he couldn't free her from the chair. Electrical tie-downs.

He raced back to the car and rooted through the glove box to find something sharp. A small pocket knife lay among the junk. By the time he'd reached Rae again and freed her, the first fire truck was swinging into the driveway.

He ignored it. They knew what to do. His priority was Rae.

"Rae?" he called softly. "Talk to me!"

She drew in a deep breath and her eyelids fluttered open. "Hunter! You're safe." She threw her arms around him.

He held her closely. "Don't worry about me. How are you?"

Rae pulled back to speak to him, but footfalls behind him stopped her. Hunter turned to see one of the firefighters approaching.

"Anyone else in there?"

"Yes! Andy!" Rae tugged on Hunter's sleeve. "I tried to drag him out, but couldn't. Kirk must have thought he'd killed him, and brought his body here to burn up with mine. He kept going on about us being fools, and Andy getting scared. Then you showed up like he expected you to, and he tried to knock —" She ended her sentence with another coughing fit.

Out of the corner of his eye, Hunter spied a firefighter quickly donning an air tank in preparation for the rescue.

Rae rolled over to her hands and knees. A moment later, weakly, she asked for some water. Hunter bolted away from her, through the unlocked front door of the house and back out after a moment. He'd grabbed a small bottle of water from her refrigerator, with the firefighters not more than twenty feet from the back of the house.

Rae drank thirstily.

Then she collapsed again, this time in Hunter's arms.

He held her tenderly, rocking her, all the while scanning the busy crowd for an ambulance. A neighbor — Hunter couldn't remember the man's name — hustled over to throw a blanket around them both.

"Thanks."

"I followed the fire truck up. This is from my car. Good thing I had it."

Rae opened her eyes at that moment, met Hunter's worried gaze and whispered, "I love you. I'm sorry I thought you'd burned down my workshop."

Behind him, Hunter heard the firefighter call to the others that he had Andy Morrison. From somewhere in the building, something caught fire with a huge *whomp.*

Rae gasped. "The fumes finally caught. The floor dried," she whispered. "God kept the fire away. . . ."

Hunter frowned, not understanding her. By now several other fire trucks had arrived. And, finally, an ambulance. In a flurry of activity, the attendants moved in, forcing him back while they checked Rae out.

Hunter backed up and watched helplessly as they worked on her.

Don't let Rae die, Lord. Don't leave me alone. Everyone else has gone and I want her so badly.

I love you, Rae. And I love You, Lord. Give her back to me, please.

"Tell us what happened," one of the attendants ordered.

He answered the man's questions woodenly, not knowing enough, and hating that he hadn't arrived even a few minutes earlier. He'd wasted precious minutes viewing those videos at the police department.

And even now, as he watched the paramedics check Rae out, he'd been thinking of his own painful past.

You needed to realize you can't do this alone. You have Jesus.

He'd dealt with his own pain, paid his and Benton's dues in the process, all alone. Time to accept it all and move on.

The attendants covered Rae's face with an oxygen mask. She opened her eyes and met Hunter's anxious stare, then lifted her hand to beckon him over.

He hurried to her side. "Hunter," she whispered, her voice hollow in the mask. "I love you. I was so scared Kirk was going after you next."

He shook his head. "It was more likely that he wanted to frame me for arson and murder."

"Don't let them blame you, Hunter. It's not fair. It wasn't fair for Dad to frame you, either."

"That's over and done with, Rae, and I'm not going to let it come between us. I'm not going to give in this time because there's a chance you may leave me. That's part of the reason I went to prison in the first place. I didn't want to care for someone who was going to leave me, as your father would have when he died."

Hunter took her hand and leaned forward to kiss her smoky hair. "I'm not going to deny us love and happiness because I'm too scared to take risks. I love you, too."

She smiled and pulled off the oxygen mask. "I'm not going to leave you."

"It looks like love is the best medicine here," the ambulance attendant said with a grin. "But we need to have a doctor give a second opinion."

"Okay," she agreed, still looking up into Hunter's eyes. "But in a minute, please."

The attendant nodded, just as a second paramedic hurried over from the burning workshop. He shook his head, his expression grim.

Rae looked up at him, her eyes wide and anxious. "Andy?"

"I'm sorry. He didn't survive. I think he'd been unconscious too long in the smoke."

She tightened her grip on Hunter's hand. "Make sure you tell the police that Kirk did this. All of it." She shook her head, her lips pursed. "I hope they find him."

A car roared up. Rae peered past Hunter. "The police are here. You have to tell them the truth. Everything. Even if it hurts people. And you have to tell Annie. She won't appreciate being lied to, not in the long run. Believe me, I know."

Hunter twisted about from his spot on the lawn. Halloway climbed out of his cruiser and walked toward them.

"They want to take Rae to the hospital," Hunter told him. "Andy Morrison is dead, and Rae says Dobson brought them both here. Thankfully, some neighbor called the fire department."

His expression grim, Halloway nodded. "Annie Dobson called, not a neighbor."

"Annie? How did she know?"

"Last night, Kirk came home drunk and boasted to her about what he was going to do. All he had to do was find you, and he told her he knew where you'd gone." Halloway slanted a speculative look at him. "She also told the dispatcher that she couldn't let you take the blame anymore. She said she was wrong about you, and that she now believes you didn't burn down the workshop ten years ago, based on what her husband said."

"My father burned it down," Rae whispered.

The officer peered at her as she sat leaning against a tree, assisted by the ambulance attendant. "There'll be an inquest," Halloway said.

Hunter shrugged as the neighbor who'd offered the blanket returned to his van. "What would it serve? I did the time, and Benton is dead. And I've already told Rae the truth. Focus your resources on finding Kirk and convicting him —"

Hunter stopped abruptly. That neighbor had arrived after him, yet a car had been parked in his driveway . . .

Had Dobson brought it? Was he still in the area?

Halloway was talking again. "Benton asked you to watch out for Rae, didn't he? That's why you came back." The man's eyebrows knitted together. "What's wrong? Is there more?"

Hunter scrubbed his face, trying to focus his thoughts.

"We'll talk later," Halloway said at his silence. "But you're going to have to come down to the station and give a full statement."

Hunter bristled as the attendants loaded Rae onto a gurney. It was one thing to bare Benton's and his sins to Rae, but doing so to Halloway was another matter. What was done was done, and the media, the police, everyone in town didn't need to hurt the Bentons.

Abruptly, a popping sound cut through the air, over the noise of engines and fire and men shouting. Halloway slumped to the ground.

Hunter grabbed the policeman, absorbing the dead weight of his body as he collapsed against him. A bloodstain spread over the officer's thigh.

Hunter's gaze flew around him. Halloway had been shot!

He spun. "Get down, everyone! Now!"

But only Rae and the ambulance attendants heard him.

Until another loud crack rang through the air.

And still another, its ricochet sparking off the gurney that held Rae. She let out a short cry.

Rae heard Hunter's shout seconds before something hot and sharp sliced through her shoulder.

She slid off the gurney and onto her knees, toppling it in the process. Thankfully, a firefighter glanced her way, and she waved madly with her good arm, to indicate they should get down, before the pain crushed her.

The man registered the warning immediately and barked out an order. All the firefighters dropped down, some crawling to take cover behind the truck.

Rae shot a desperate look toward Hunter, who was dragging Halloway behind the ambulance.

"Rae?"

She answered Hunter's shout. "I'm okay!" When the firing stopped, she turned to the attendant beside her. "Just help Halloway."

Rae's heart pounded. The gurney had saved her life. She could see the fresh scrape where the bullet had ricocheted off the bar to graze her shoulder, which stung madly.

Hunter yelled out, "Stay there, Rae! Kirk's in the woods."

She obeyed, but not before peering through the trees at the far side of the well lit yard, anxious to catch —

There, a movement! What had Kirk been wearing? She dug through the jumbled mess of her memory, until she remembered. Dark green. Work clothes, something that would camouflage well.

But the rifle stood out, too perfect, too straight amid the tangled forest around it.

She snagged Hunter's attention. "There he is! To the left of the fire!"

Hunter vaulted over the wounded officer and the ambulance attendant and ran into the woods. With that movement, Kirk would be distracted. Taking advantage of it, Rae raced over to where Halloway lay prone on the ground, the other attendant following. Both medics worked feverishly on the wounded policeman.

Rae looked around for Hunter. When she tried to call out to him, her throat refused to cooperate.

"Be quiet. Get down."

She turned to the source of the raspy voice. Halloway swallowed, obviously in pain, gripping his leg. "If you call out, you could risk tipping off the shooter. Get down."

Rae glanced up at the attendants, then at Halloway. "But no one knows the trails like I do. I know where he's going!"

"Just stay down." Halloway sat up straighter. "Back-up's on its way, and if Hunter can chase Dobson away from here, we can get to safety faster."

"Kirk knows the woods, too. The ravine's riddled with small caves and hiding spots. Hunter's walking into a trap!"

"Forget it! Stay here!"

"No!" She shook her head. "Hunter has done so much for my family. I won't turn my back on him now."

Refusing to wait for Halloway's answer, she scrambled to the edge of the nearest truck, where two firefighters were still crouching. With only a cursory glance at her burning workshop, she dashed across the yard and into the woods.

Rae found a trail immediately. Years ago, she and her friends had made many of them, leading from the house to several small caves. It had been ages since she'd taken them, but the landscape was permanently mapped in her head.

Stopping at the edge of one sharp drop off, she squatted down and listened. The noises of the fire and commotion at her home, piggybacked on the thick smoke, blotted out her painful wheezing.

But it also blotted out any sounds made by Hunter and Kirk.

In the light from the fire, she spied movement to her right and downward. Both men were moving. She knew exactly where Kirk was leading Hunter.

A small cave, perfect for an ambush.

She swung her legs over the ledge and dropped, scraping through forest debris as she slid down the gully. When she threw out her arm to steady herself, pain shot through her shoulder.

The cave was ahead, and Kirk swiftly tucked himself into it. His back was to her. Beyond, approaching him, was Hunter.

Walking right into a trap.

At just the right moment, she slipped behind a tree and called out, "Kirk!"

He swung around, his rifle high and ready. She stayed still, hopefully hidden by the bushy evergreen.

Suddenly, Hunter leaped into view and onto Kirk. The rifle tumbled from Dobson's hands. Both men hit the ground, Hunter landing on top. With one effective swing, he knocked Kirk out for the count.

Rae rushed up to them. Hunter drew in a breath, climbed off Kirk and pulled the groggy man up.

Pounding feet through the brush drew Rae's attention away from Hunter, and she pivoted. A police officer, then another, slid down the short cliff toward them.

"You didn't kill him, did you?" one of the officers asked.

As if in answer, Kirk lifted his head and groaned.

"No." Hunter released the man, who flopped to the ground. The officers took over, moving Kirk out of the way, handcuffing him and making the journey back up the hillside along the path instead of the sheer rock face Rae had slid down.

Hunter stepped back, nodding when they told him he'd need to come to the station, too, shaking his head when they asked if he was hurt.

All the while, though, he kept his gaze focused on Rae. "I'm sorry, Rae," he said then. "I did exactly what your father didn't want me to do."

Her knees buckled, and she felt weak and watery at the sight of his pained expression. Instantly, he rushed toward her, catching her in his arms so she wouldn't fall.

She clung to him. "Dad didn't want you to fight for nothing, but to fight for something important. Like this."

A light dawned in Hunter's eyes, and he brushed the leaves and needles from her clothes. She smiled. "And he wanted me to forgive you. You know, it's so easy to do that."

Hunter dropped a light kiss onto her face. "That's the power of a God-given love."

TWENTY-ONE

Hunter pulled up the chair from the corner of the hospital bed and gave it to Rae. She sat down across from where Halloway rested, and adjusted the sling that supported her injured arm.

"When will you get out of here?" she asked the officer. It had been two days since they'd been shot. Her wound was superficial. His was far more serious.

Halloway flicked the IV. "As soon as my blood work comes back normal. One small reaction to a drug and they hook you up to every gizmo going."

"It's for your own good," she said, smiling.

The man returned the smile before looking up at Hunter. "Hey, thanks for all you did back there."

"You'd have done the same."

"Looks like I owe you twice."

Hunter felt Rae's eyes on him. "Go on,

Hunter, tell him," she said.

"Rae, he isn't interested in that."

"But it's good news. Everyone should hear it."

Hunter gave her an indulgent smile. Halloway looked back and forth between the two. "Tell me what?"

"Hunter found his family."

"A brother," he corrected. "He's been living here in Moncton for years. He saw my face on TV, and heard the last name."

"He was adopted shortly after birth, and his parents told him that was his original name," Rae interjected. "With some checking, they discovered he's Hunter's older brother."

"That's great!" Halloway said, nodding.

Hunter gave Rae another indulgent smile. "And he wants to come to our wedding."

Halloway laughed. "The good news keeps on coming."

They all chuckled. Then, after a moment of silence, Halloway shifted into a more comfortable position. "I'm not supposed to comment on an investigation, Hunter," he said quietly. "But let me say a few things. We knew Morrison had someone else with him. We just didn't know who. And the rezoning came at just the right time to catch him.

"That's why the police brought in my wife, against my wishes, I might add. But Christine wanted to help, and yes, I'll admit she had the expertise and the determination to be an asset." He glanced at Rae. "As soon as we found out that your father was involved, and that he had cancer, I visited him in the hospital. I gave him the opportunity to come clean."

She leaned forward. "I saw you leaving, just as I was arriving. What did he tell you?"

"He was delirious. He mentioned Kirk, but his pain medication was making him confused. We weren't even sure he'd said Kirk's name."

Rae shivered. "Kirk must have had money up front to buy the land. Andy didn't, and Dad must have backed out."

"Dobson remortgaged his house without Annie's consent. He forged her name on the papers. He figured if he bought the government land, got yours and sold the whole lot to investors, he'd have enough to retire someplace safe.

"He would have been successful, too," Halloway continued, shifting again. "But Andy Morrison wanted to change tactics, and that was why Dobson tried to kill him. A unique plan . . .

"Morrison went to Dobson after he retrieved his car, to confront him. There, he was knocked out and dumped in Dobson's old smokehouse. The day he attacked you, Dobson decided that was the perfect opportunity to kill him and frame you. Except that Morrison didn't die, but rather returned to confront him, we believe."

Rae nodded. "Kirk had it all figured out, even using his old smokehouse. He and Dad used to smoke herring and deer jerky in it."

"He had planned to frame Hunter for the fire, and me for the brake tampering. We found Dobson's fingerprints on the Dumpster and on Morrison's belt. He dumped the bloody clothing there and said he'd seen Hunter do it." Halloway blew out a sigh. "He was as greedy as Morrison. And about as smart."

Rae shook her head. "Kirk said he was careful because he'd watched all those crime shows on TV."

"Well, he wasn't careful enough."

"Those two were so greedy," she murmured.

"We should thank Annie," Hunter interjected. "She was strong enough to do the right thing."

"I've been speaking with her," Rae said softly. "She'd suspected things for some time, but it wasn't until Dad died that she realized how people should put things right while they're still alive. All she'd been doing was praying about it, hoping the Lord would change Kirk's heart. When he came home drunk and boasted to her about it, she decided to act. She said prayer is wonderful, but action is needed, too, something she'd been reluctant to do."

Rae glanced at Hunter before adding, "At some time, Kirk attacked Andy and tried to frame you for murder. With Morrison acting like my boyfriend, everyone would assume you'd become jealous and killed him." She scowled. "I believe he tried to kill my father, in fact. Soaking those rags in the shop, and then putting a dangerous sealant on the propane stove. But at some point, he must have decided to wait for Dad to die. When you arrived, Hunter, he saw a different way to get the land."

Halloway murmured, "This is going to be a rough time for your cousin. Fortunately, she's willing to testify against Kirk. Based on some other evidence, we believe your father has given half of his insurance money to charity."

"We never did find it," Rae said pensively. "But what amazes me is seeing God's love for us in all of this."

Hunter looked down at her, and saw Rae's

eyes were glistening. "Enough. We can discuss it later." He pulled her up and hugged her close. "This conversation will keep for another day. But you won't. I take the job of keeping you safe very seriously. Oh, which reminds me, Mike. I'm turning down that job offer. We've decided to rebuild Benton Woodworking, again. I believe it's what God wants us to do. And Rae just heard that a new community is going to be built on the north side of the highway. The investors didn't like how difficult the rezoning was becoming. So we keep our forest and I should have lots of work."

She kissed Hunter lightly, shyly. "Am I just a job to you?"

He kissed her back. "A labor of love. I read in my Bible last night about labor prompted by love."

"To encourage new believers." She grinned. "And ones like us who are still learning a lot."

Dear Reader,

Prejudice is a difficult topic, isn't it? We all have some in varying degrees, but I think it's how we deal with it that makes us good citizens. In *Keeping Her Safe*, I dealt with preconceived notions, mostly from my heroine, about prison life, and those on the fringe of society. But my hero, Hunter Gordon, had his own prejudices. He assumed that he would be abandoned by all he loved. That was why he wouldn't get close to the heroine, Rae.

But if we let Him, God can show us that He loves us all equally, and He can show us how to set aside preconceived notions and ideas. Remember that if Jesus died for us, He also died for those against whom we have bias. In my story, Rae is shown that, through patient, loving Christians like Hunter and his cellmate, Louis. But sometimes we don't have that luxury. We just have to remember that God made us all, and He never makes mistakes.

Bless you!
Barbara Phinney

QUESTIONS FOR DISCUSSION

1. Did you find some prejudice on Rae's part at the beginning of the story? At the end? What changed her mind?

2. Rae feels sorry for herself after she has been attacked in her home, even asking Hunter why she's suffering. He tells her about Job. Does he do the right thing? What would you say if you were asked that?

3. Rae doesn't believe Hunter when he says she's in danger. What would you do? What do you think is the best way for a Christian to act, both in Hunter's and in Rae's position?

4. Hunter called Rae a modern-day Job, but do you think that in some ways, Hunter

was the real modern-day Job? Why or why not?

5. Hunter also feels sorry for himself, but in a way that makes him sensitive to prejudice. Why? What should he have done to handle this?

6. When something frightening has happened to you, is your first reaction one of prayer? What might you have prayed for if you were in Rae's situation?

7. If prayer wouldn't be your first resort in a frightening situation, what are some ways you can remedy that and begin to pray thankfully during desperate times?

8. Do you think it was right for Hunter to withhold the truth about Rae's father? Dowe, too often, kill the messenger? How can we accept truth without getting upset?

9. Hunter finally decides not to accept the bad things that happened to him, and becomes determined not to take the blame for the second fire, even if only in his mind. Do you think Christians should fight? What are your biblical references for

your answer?

10. Consider how, because the workshop floor was damp from the rainy weather and Hunter cleaning it, that it helped to keep the gas from igniting in the last chapter. God's hand is evident in this story, but it's just a work of fiction. Have you ever seen God's hand in something in your life? Explain.

11. Rae feels the touch of the Holy Spirit through her guilty conscience. Eventually, it prompts her to pay for the cottage. What other examples of this are there in *Keeping Her Safe*?

12. When the Holy Spirit prompts Rae, she acts on it, such as apologizing to Hunter. This is extremely hard not only for her, but Hunter, too. How can we make it easier in our own lives, when we must apologize?

ABOUT THE AUTHOR

Barbara Phinney was born in England and raised in Canada. She has traveled throughout her life, loving to explore the various countries and cultures of the world. After she retired from the Canadian Armed Forces, Barbara turned her hand to romance writing. The thrill of adventure and the love of happy endings, coupled with a too-active imagination, have merged to help her create this and other wonderful stories. Barbara spends her days writing, building her dream home with her husband and enjoying their fast-growing children.

The employees of Thorndike Press hope you have enjoyed this Large Print book. All our Thorndike, Wheeler, and Kennebec Large Print titles are designed for easy reading, and all our books are made to last. Other Thorndike Press Large Print books are available at your library, through selected bookstores, or directly from us.

For information about titles, please call:
(800) 223-1244

or visit our Web site at:
http://gale.cengage.com/thorndike

To share your comments, please write:
Publisher
Thorndike Press
295 Kennedy Memorial Drive
Waterville, ME 04901